USA Today BESTSELLING AUTHOR

Dale Mayer

TERK'S GUARDIANS

WALLACE 14

WALLACE: TERK'S GUARDIANS, BOOK 14
Beverly Dale Mayer
Valley Publishing Ltd.

ISBN-13: 978-1-778867-02-6
Print Edition

Books in This Series:

About This Book

Wallace wasn't sure why he'd answered Jonas's call to discuss setting up a unit akin to Terk's remarkable team. Perhaps it was curiosity or something more. But, as soon as he lands in England, he's thrust into a crisis. One of the MI6 research applicants has vanished, and Jonas fears the worst. Then Wallace hears her name …

Amy, an old friend of Terk's, had been swept into peril without warning. Captured—with no clue as to where she was, why she was taken, or by whom—she manages to send a desperate message to Terk. Only when she connects with him mentally does her panic transform into steely determination. Whoever is behind this will pay. She wasn't alone anymore. She has powerful allies. Allies who, even now, were racing to her aid, … she hoped.

For Wallace, finding Amy becomes an urgent mission, and ensuring her safe return is a close second. But what seems like a straightforward rescue quickly spirals into a tangled web of danger and intrigue. Amid the chaos, an unexpected connection sparks between them again, adding a layer of complexity to their perilous journey, as the stakes become more personal than ever.

Sign up to be notified of all Dale's releases here!
https://geni.us/DaleNews

PROLOGUE

T ERK LOOKED UP with interest as the newcomers arrived at the dining room table. He recognized the appetite for a fulfilling relationship and the cementing of their energy-worker bond, and he nodded. "Welcome," he greeted them. "Your rooms are ready, whenever you want to take your luggage up. If you're staying here, that is, as I understand Morrison has a place close by."

Sadie sat down across from Terk and reached out for a handshake, as she smiled. "Thank you."

He gave her a gentle smile in return, shaking her hand. "What are you thanking me for?" he asked, amusement rippling through his tone.

"I don't know whether it should be for giving me a place to stay, for the support I've needed, for the help with my brothers, or for tossing Morrison in my direction."

"For all that, you are welcome. Besides you have talents that could use some honing and ones we want to learn more about, so it's a good trade-off.

She realized for the first time that there really was a profound sense of connection and community here. But she would learn more, and she would understand more.

Just then Terk's phone rang. He groaned as he reached for his phone and asked, "Jonas, what's up?"

"I need two men right now," he snapped, "as in today."

"Depends on where you are."

"I'm in London, and I need somebody right now."

"As in twenty minutes from now?"

"Preferably ten minutes from now," he added urgently. "I have one guy here who told me to call you to get backup, but I don't know if he's one of yours or not."

"Who is it?" Terk asked curiously, as he looked around the dining room table, knowing that most of his men were here, though a few were still off on jobs.

"His name is Wallace."

At that Terk stiffened. "Wallace Cremayne?"

Muffled voices came from the other end of the call, and a new voice came on board. "Hey, Terk. Wallace here. Jonas has a problem."

"Jonas always has a problem," Terk noted. "What are you doing there?"

"I came over because they wanted to talk to me about bringing up a unit similar to what you were doing for the CIA," he explained. "They figured that you were too big and too government-shy to want to do it."

"So, they contacted you?" Terk asked in amusement. "I guess they didn't look into your history too much."

"Nope, they sure didn't, but, while we were here, one of the researchers that they were also trying to hire has disappeared."

At that, Terk closed his eyes, pinched the bridge of his nose, and got straight to the point. "Don't tell me it's Amy."

"Yeah, it's Amy," Wallace confirmed. "Amy Connelly. I'm going after her, but I don't know what we'll need. Jonas is asking for two backups, but, honest to God, if I even had one, I would be happy."

More chatter came in the background, and then Riff

joined the call.

"Hey, Terk. I'm here in London already, so I can handle this. You guys enjoy setting up home for the latest newcomers." And, with that, Riff was gone, and the call ended.

Terk stared down at the phone and then looked at the others gathered at the table with him. "That was interesting. Riff's in London, where Wallace was doing something for Jonas, but apparently Amy's disappeared, and we need all hands on deck for this one."

"Amy?" Several of the women looked at each other, then back at Terk.

He nodded. "Somebody I knew as a kid. You guys probably don't know her, but Merk and I do. Damn, I'll need to tell Merk. If Levi's got anybody to help, maybe we can get him to pinch-hit, as needed." Then he frowned and tapped the table, as premonitions started filtering through his brain. "Well, shit, she's been kidnapped, and they want her to do research for them, but I don't know who it is. I'm definitely feeling …" Then he frowned. "I feel as if Asia's coming into this somehow."

"From London to Asia?" Celia asked.

He shrugged. "Or big money, as in China maybe? I don't know." Terk shook his head. "But they need help, and we need to help them now."

CHAPTER 1

WALLACE CREMAYNE STUDIED the huge MI6 offices, as he waited impatiently for Jonas to return. He checked his phone once again to see whether anybody had had any direct communication from Amy or had found any indirect messages buried in the internet. He shook his head.

Wallace had already spoken with Terk's brother, Merk, asking for his help—and the loan of Levi's satellite—to scour social media and the dark web, looking for any communications that even eluded to a psychic researcher being for hire—or kidnapping someone with energy-working abilities. That would be a big ongoing project, so nothing had been found yet. However, if anything popped up, they would let Wallace know immediately.

Before Merk ended the call, he suggested, "Could be big money financing the kidnappings of these gifted people. As Terk mentioned, could be anywhere in Asia. Could even be foreign governments. For that matter, could be our own government. We all know what happened to Terk and his team."

Wallace groaned when hearing that.

Merk continued. "So, do what you do best. In the meantime, we'll look for cryptic language that may lead to Amy."

Wallace again checked his phone and sighed.

He and Amy had connected after landing in London,

once they realized just what the British government wanted them to do for MI6. They stayed in contact, until she failed to show up this morning.

He'd waited for her and then asked Jonas about her, who suggested she must be running late. Yet, when she didn't show up hours later, Wallace went to the hotel to see what was going on, hoping that nothing had gone wrong. He hoped to find her there, ready and waiting. Instead the hotel shared that she hadn't returned the previous night and that her security key hadn't been used since Wallace had last seen her. So somewhere after eight o'clock—when they finished a business dinner with several others, then dropped her off at her hotel—she had gone missing.

Considering her hotel room was on the third floor—and she hadn't made it past the front entrance—was beyond concerning. The added fact that nobody knew she was missing until now also meant that whomever or whatever had happened in between gave the bad guys a major head start, definitely leaving the good guys at a disadvantage.

Wallace stood up as soon as Jonas appeared, introducing the man with him as Riff. He had offered no other name, which was so damn typical of people in this field, particularly when they were more like Terk than Jonas. They all headed into Jonas's office, as Riff argued fiercely with Jonas. Finally Riff just slashed his hand out in a motion, suggesting that the conversation was over.

He turned to Wallace. "You ready to go?"

Wallace nodded. "Past ready. Do we have a destination?"

"The hotel."

"But we checked there," Jonas snapped at Riff again.

"Of course you checked," Riff muttered, his tone flat, "but what you look for and may or may not find is nothing like what we'll be looking for."

Jonas hesitated, eyeing them. "You really think you'll find something?"

"Yes, we do, but we have to get there first, and you need to clear it, stat."

"It's cleared," Jonas confirmed, his tone grumpy, "but I don't have time to run around and do this."

"It's better if you're not with us anyway," Riff stated. "So, stay here and do what you do. We'll follow up." With a smile, he added, "We're taking the government rig though. It does give us a little bit of panache."

"Not really." Jonas groaned. "It will probably bring you nothing but trouble."

"You could be right," Riff agreed, with a cheerful smile, "but we need wheels now." And, with that, he gave a nod to Wallace. "Let's get out of here."

They quickly walked away from Jonas, knowing that he knew how to play the game. Even if Jonas struggled with somebody else calling the shots, he wasn't questioning them, … at least not much.

Riff took the driver's seat. As Wallace got into the passenger seat, he asked, "Will this backfire on us?"

"Not with Jonas, never," he replied, with a shrug. "Jonas has to play within the parameters of his government job," Riff explained. "We don't and we won't. Jonas is well accustomed to keeping us out of trouble, yet he also knows that this deal is bad news for everybody. Once it gets ugly, there really are no happy endings, not until we get to the bottom of it. He will do everything he can to cover us, but he can't just give us a government vehicle. However, if I took it? … That's a different story. Same thing regarding clearance to get into the hotel. Great if we have it, but, if we don't, we'll take it anyway." He glanced at Wallace. "Jonas can cover us for what we've done but can't give us permission for a great deal of what we do because it's beyond the scope of what his mandate will allow."

"Right." Wallace gave a headshake. "Government and all."

"Absolutely," Riff confirmed, with a smirk. "Government and all. It's tough on everybody, but we all play it this way because we have to."

Wallace understood that.

"What the hell is this I hear about you coming over to MI6 for a job?" Riff asked him curiously.

"They dangled in front of me this concept of setting up something similar to what Terk had going with the CIA," he shared a bit sheepishly. "So, I came over to check it out. Amy was brought in for interviews as well. I don't really know for sure, but, at this point, I'm wondering if we were set up."

Riff fell silent as he considered that. "If somebody was curious as to what you guys were up to—and especially if they didn't know that you had these kinds of abilities—coming in for this MI6 job interview just made an announcement to the big wide world."

"Yet nobody was supposed to even know about the interview or the job, not to mention what the team would do. Neither was there any public knowledge as to what we can do."

"But it's government," Riff noted, with a headshake. "Which really just means, everybody in the government knows."

"It's supposed to be Black Ops–level containment," Wallace grumbled.

"And to a certain extent it will be. However, if they've

got somebody against all this or somebody being paid to find out information, then this intel is huge," he muttered. "You can't ever trust the government."

"No, but I was thinking that Jonas's group might be different."

"Was it actually Jonas who brought you over?"

Wallace frowned, then shook his head. "No, you're right there. It wasn't him. It was implied, and I inferred, that he was involved, but nobody ever came out and stated it was his deal."

"And because they didn't say that outright, I wouldn't trust it," Riff pointed out.

"Damn," Wallace swore under his breath.

"How well do you know Amy?"

"I used to know her very well," he shared, with a smile. "At one point in time we had a bit of a thing, but neither of us were ready for commitment back then. When I realized she was here for her interview, I was happy to see her again. I got pretty excited. She's quite powerful in her own way, but I'd heard that she had been severely ill not all that long ago. So, if she was here, I took that to mean she was back on her feet, including with access to her abilities."

"What abilities?"

"Remember that I haven't seen in her years. Last I knew of her skills, I would call her this navigation efficiency expert. Don't know what she calls it. She can look at a map and can pretty well plan out where to go, how to go, and has a great deal of success in getting there without traffic lights, delays on planes, and anything going awry." He shrugged. "It's marvelous. Not necessarily the most useful thing in terms of government programs though because I believe it only works if she's doing the traveling."

Riff took his gaze off the road to glance at Wallace. "That would be freaking awesome if each of us could do that."

"It would. She and I both left the USA at the same time for this interview, and she got to England a hell of a lot faster than I did. Jonas did look a little confused at the initial meet."

"Of course, being Jonas," Riff muttered, "he's also got to keep his own agenda moving forward."

"Does he have his own agenda?" Wallace asked him.

"They all do. That you can count on. One way or another, they all do. As far as government types go, we trust Jonas as much as anybody, but when push comes to shove? … I don't think we'll ever get precedence over his work. So, keep that in mind. If it'll get him in trouble, there is a limit to things he can help you with."

"Of course there is," Wallace noted, with a wry tone. "There's always a limit. It's just never quite the same as what we think the limits should be."

"*Right.*" Riff gave him a wry smile. "Not a surprise when you put it that way. It's just one of those things we have to look at."

"Okay, I got it, but meanwhile …"

"Exactly, meanwhile, we need to find her." Riff shifted lanes, merging smoothly into traffic. "We went years searching for energy workers before we had anybody who even came close to being skilled, and now it seems as if, everywhere I turn, I'm coming up against them."

"I think the more you have to do with Terk, the more you see them," Wallace suggested, with a smirk. "In Amy's case, I wasn't even sure where her abilities were at, after her illness."

"Why would being sick affect your abilities?"

Wallace looked over at him. "When you think about it, *not* being sick means you're at full energy."

"Good point," Riff replied.

At the hotel, they parked away from the heavy traffic area and hopped out. As they walked inside, Riff suggested to Wallace, "You can go to the reception desk, if you want, but I'm heading straight to the room first."

"Then I'm with you," Wallace replied.

They bypassed the front desk, and nobody stopped them.

Riff shrugged. "That's fairly typical. As long as you act like you know what you're doing and where you're going, nobody really gives a crap."

"Yet we have a missing woman," Wallace muttered. "Shouldn't somebody care?"

"Somebody should care, but too often nobody does," Riff stated. "Remember that."

Feeling as if he had just heard some lecture on the underbelly of the universe, Wallace nodded and kept on walking. In a way it was true, and a sad truth, since so often people didn't care. As long as you acted with authority and intent, nobody questioned you. But now that they had a missing woman, surely he and Riff should talk to people, to potential witnesses. Yet Wallace presumed MI6 had already done so. Or MI5, depending on where they thought this kidnapping was going.

He frowned at that and asked Riff, "Is there any coordination between MI5 and MI6?"

"Sometimes." Riff gave him a lopsided grin. "How much coordination and communication do you think there is between any two government departments?"

Wallace sighed. "You would think there would at least be weekly meetings or something."

"Nope, not happening. On the other hand, if Jonas is spearheading the investigation, then rest assured that we will get the cooperation of both."

"Even though he's MI6?"

"Yep, absolutely." Riff smiled. "We do have some advantages to having Jonas on our side of the table."

"I would think so, but it needs to be a big-enough advantage to make a difference," he murmured. "We really do need a break on this."

At the door to Amy's hotel room, Riff stopped, looked around, pondered.

"What are you thinking?" Wallace asked him.

"I'm wondering when her room was last cleaned and if they saw anything."

"Chances are, it wasn't cleaned because she wasn't due to check out yet, but ..."

"Right, *but* we can't count on that."

"Nope, we sure can't," Wallace confirmed. "I can track down maid service—unless it's the same people who worked yesterday ..."

"Exactly," Riff agreed. "Let's check out the room first." And, with that, Riff let himself into the room.

A moment later, Wallace realized that Riff didn't have a key, and Wallace saw no lockpicks used either. He tucked away that bit of information in the back of his head. As he walked into the hotel room, they both stopped, and Wallace frowned. "Cold, empty, no energy at all. Is this even her room?" he asked, curiously looking around. "It doesn't feel like her room."

"I know. It doesn't feel like anybody's room." Riff

frowned, as he looked around. "If this was her room, I don't think she ever stayed in it."

"I agree with you there," Wallace replied. "And, if it wasn't her room, then why were we told it was?"

"Exactly."

Frowning at that, he turned to Riff. "I'll head back down to the front desk and double-check the information we got."

Riff just nodded.

Wallace quickly headed for the elevators, and a few minutes later was at the main reception area. He explained to the desk clerk just who he was and why he was here. He explained how there appeared to be some mix-up, and they were given the wrong room number.

The woman frowned at him. "That's what I have on the registry." She clicked on the computer keys, bringing up the registration.

"Then she obviously changed her room," Wallace suggested.

The woman shook her head, while she read the notes on the computer, then exclaimed, "She did. You're right. I am so sorry for the mix-up."

"Good, so what room was she in then?" he asked, sounding harsher than he intended.

The clerk checked a few other screens and then replied, "Fifth floor. Room 512. I'm so sorry for the mix-up."

"Was a reason given for why she changed rooms?" He studied the clerk. "Did you ever see her?"

She shook her head. "No, I haven't seen her myself. So I haven't checked her in or out."

"Right now, as far as we're concerned, she's missing."

"But maybe she's in the other room."

"Would you not have had that information to give the

cops in the first place?" he asked, getting frustrated.

She frowned and nodded. "We should have, yes. So I don't understand why we didn't."

"And that is my concern. If 512 is her room, then why did everybody else get sent to a different room? This can't be a simple mistake."

"I see a notation that her room was changed at her request, but I don't see a reason why."

"Not that a reason is necessarily an issue, but the fact that she made a request and that you gave it to her is good. Yet, when the cops contacted you, they should have been directed to the new room that she was checked into. The fact that the cops weren't given that info raises questions, serious questions." Wallace sighed. More research to do, including deep background checks into all the employees in this hotel, whether part-time or full-time, then cross-referencing their friends and family. Levi and Terk may both need to be on this project.

"I don't know why, sir. You are absolutely correct, but I can offer no explanation." She kept apologizing over and over, but the conversation wasn't going anywhere.

He finally held up a hand to her. "Stop. Our people will check into that. Can you just give me the correct room key? I need to check that room."

She seemed distraught as she handed over the key.

Wallace headed to the elevator, already texting Levi and Terk with his latest need for more research. He went straight up to the fifth floor, now texting Riff about the room change and to meet up here.

At the door to Amy's actual room, Wallace used the key and let himself in. Inside the room, he noted the energy. Unfortunately it was all the wrong kind. Because this room hadn't been mentioned initially to the cops, the assumption had been made that Amy had been missing since she had been dropped off. However, now it seemed more likely that she had had a visitor, who had completely destroyed the room, looking for something or just wanting to destroy things.

He phoned the front desk and asked when the door to 512 had last been opened.

After a few keystrokes, the clerk stated that the room was opened at 11:15 last night. When he asked when it had opened afterward, she replied in a concerned voice, "I don't have anything else here, not until you just entered the room only minutes ago."

"So, you're saying that it was opened at 11:15 p.m., and I presume she left at that hour and was she alone?"

"I don't know," the clerk admitted, her tone nervous. "All I can tell you is that, according to the computer, the room was accessed at 11:15 p.m., and that's all."

"And to access security camera footage?" he asked.

"You'll need the manager for that."

Thanking her, he ended the call.

The only way a kidnapping could happen was if Amy had opened the door to somebody, who promptly knocked her out. Then propped open the door, so her intruder could destroy the place—or could make it look as if they were destroying it. Thereafter, the kidnapper picked up Amy and took her away, letting the door close at that time.

If that was what really happened—and it was a big *if*—this sucked.

As he stood here, Riff walked in behind him and whistled. "What happened here?"

"At 11:15 last night somebody accessed her room, but

the door hasn't been opened since then, not until I came in just now."

"We think she opened her door willingly?"

"If it's just the one time instance—and that's what the desk clerk is saying—then Amy obviously let somebody in, or at least opened the door, thinking it was somebody she needed to talk to." Wallace gave a wave of his hand. "What we're looking at then is that somebody possibly came in at that time and snagged her but destroyed the room to make it appear that a burglary or an argument or something happened here. Then they somehow managed to get Amy out of here at the same time."

"So, we also need to check the elevators at that time period," Riff suggested, looking around. "We need to see who may have knocked her out and took her away."

"That's what I'm thinking," Wallace said, staring at the room. "Definitely energy is here, but it's just not energy I like."

"There's nothing about it I like," Riff declared. "This feels as if there was a struggle, a woman fighting for herself, for her life, and I won't say she lost her life, but she certainly lost her freedom."

With that, Wallace turned and headed back downstairs, looking for the security camera feeds from last night. It took a little bit longer to get a manager and to get the clearance to bring up that footage. As soon as they had it, he watched as a cleaning cart rolled down the hallway, and the maid in a uniform stopped at Amy's door, as if to hand over extra towels, and the laundry hamper was pushed in. When it was pushed back out again, it headed back down toward the same service elevator and then disappeared.

When he asked for cameras for the service elevator, it

was a no-go. "Sorry, we don't have any of those," the manager replied. "They're literally just for workers."

"Of course it's for workers, but maybe your workers are involved in this kidnapping ring. Did you consider that?" he asked in frustration. The manager frowned and shook his head. Wallace continued. "I've already got a team doing a deep dive into all your employees and their known associates. Meanwhile, you guys can explain to MI6 why you don't have cameras in this area and why a guest the government brought in was kidnapped from your hotel at that hour, and you don't have any record of it."

The manager paled and panicked. "It is something that we're in the process of getting," he offered, "but nothing's been set up yet."

"Where does the service elevator go?"

"It stops at every floor, but it also goes down to the laundry area." With that, the manager led Wallace down to the laundry room, part of the basement. Wallace sent a text to update Riff and harbored a faint hope that Amy might still be unconscious in a laundry hamper somewhere nearby. However, a thorough search of the area didn't reveal such a simple answer. Riff showed up and joined them now that they were done searching. A grim expression on his face, Wallace looked over at his partner.

Riff nodded in concern. "Nothing is here, absolutely no sign of where she's gone or when. We'll head out to the parking lot, check street cameras, any hotel cams," he added, turning to look at the manager, who shook his head. Riff turned to Wallace. "We'll have to check anything around that 11:15 p.m. time."

Taking their leave, they returned to their vehicle and phoned Jonas, wanting access to local street cams, hoping to use Jonas's supercomputer.

Jonas sighed. "Sure, I can get you access, but the kidnappers may have avoided being seen on any of them already. Considering Amy had appointments this morning with MI6, we would know to worry when she didn't show up. Still, taking her at 11:15 p.m. gave them at least a nine-hour head start, which was probably planned."

"Do we get access or not?" Riff asked.

Jonas groaned. "Yes. I'm just telling you that it'll end up being a waste of your time. Still, give me some time to set up a secure spot for you to work from, where no one will bother you or will know what you're doing either. I'm sure you'll find something useful to do in the meantime."

"Definitely something is going on here that we aren't seeing," Wallace declared, "and we need to. Otherwise there's a chance Amy won't see the light of day again."

With that, he ended the call.

WALLACE AND RIFF remained in the MI6 rig, in the hotel parking lot, planning out their next move. "I presume Terk has been in contact with her," Wallace shared with Riff.

Riff quickly dialed Terk and asked him, putting him on Speakerphone.

"Amy has no idea what happened, no idea where she is, even wondering if this wasn't some twisted job interview to see what she could do." Terk's tone was hardened with disbelief.

At that, Riff's eyebrows shot up, and he stared at Wallace. "I might have thought that myself, if I was locked up as she's apparently been."

Terk agreed. "Especially when she was picked up from her room, doesn't know who took her, doesn't know anything about it. So far, she's met one captor, and they are feeding her, but she's lost time, so they're obviously drugging her," Terk shared.

Wallace sighed. "That makes sense, and it also keeps her compliant, dulls her gifts." Wallace hated the idea, but what if she was right about a twisted job interview? The thought pissed him off, but it was all too possible.

Terk added, "She's waiting for somebody to arrive but doesn't know who or what to expect. For the moment, they're treating her okay. She believes she's in London—or at least that's what she was told. I'll stay in touch with her for as long as I can and will keep you updated." Then Terk ended the call.

"If they're not lying to her and if she really is in London, that would be a very good thing," Riff replied, with a nod. "Terk does have a locator on his staff, so I bet he's getting Langdon in on this."

"If a locator does just that, then I would imagine so," Wallace said. "Yet you never really know because not everybody can turn it on and off all the time. Plus, certain buildings can block our energy."

Riff nodded. "In addition to your two points, in this case, where we have so much added pressure as one of our own was taken, our energy work doesn't always hold up to the stress factor."

Wallace faced Riff. "How come nobody from the government has gotten back to us on the street cams? That seems a bit dodgy."

"Because we asked for their help," Riff replied, with a wry look. "Also because somebody in-house may be involved in Amy's kidnapping. … You do know this would go a lot faster without them, right?"

"In that case, let's do it without them," Wallace stated.

"Good." Riff snorted. "Let's jump in and do this. I do better without any of them looking over my shoulder."

Wallace glared at him. "If you had a better idea right from the beginning, why didn't you say so?"

"I did, but you were still thinking this wasn't necessarily a big deal."

"Wait. I've always considered it a big deal," he declared, staring at Riff. "Amy's not here, and I assume it wasn't her choice to leave, but I was hardly expecting a drugged kidnapping of a potential MI6 hire. That's pretty brazen."

"That's the thing about government work," Riff noted. "You can't ever really count on anything. So you *never* know what to expect. I wouldn't put it past MI6 to be putting her through a test. If that is not enough for you, look at the job you guys were being asked to do."

Wallace nodded. "Not a bad theory," he admitted. "I sure hope Amy's wrong about that though because if we can't trust Jonas …"

"Yeah, well, in a way, I would hope that she's right because then, chances are, we'll get her out of this in one piece. However, if it's a private contract, and somebody else is looking at her skills, wondering what she can or can't do, that's a whole different story. If she fails, … who says she'll get a free pass to just walk out."

"No, they won't take that kindly, will they?"

"They never do," Riff said, his tone hard. "These people, if not MI6, will have a very different take on this scenario."

"So, how do we find out if it is or is not an MI6 trial run?" Wallace asked, staring at Riff.

"I don't generally deal with governments. I avoid them like the plague," he shared cheerfully. "Mostly because of shit like this."

"You think her theory has merit?"

"Of course it has merit," he stated, frowning at Wallace. "Didn't we just say that?"

"I guess it just feels wrong to think that the *British* government would do that."

"Wrong maybe, but when it comes to Special Ops, Black Ops? … Hell no. They pull this shit all the time."

Such vehemence filled Riff's tone that Wallace had absolutely no doubt that, as far as Riff was concerned, it was totally possible. Still, it was a little unnerving to consider. Wallace wasn't at all sure he was ready to jump on the same *hating of governments* bandwagon that Riff was on.

Riff grabbed his duffel bag from the back seat and pulled out his laptop. "Let's hack into MI6's street cams."

Wallace nodded, grabbing his laptop too. Two hours later, he shook his head. "Jonas may be right. They avoided all the street cams."

"*And*," Riff added, "Jonas has still not called us back."

"Are you thinking what I'm thinking?" Wallace asked.

"Damn straight. Let's go have a face-to-face chat with Jonas."

Riff and Wallace left the hotel parking lot and shortly pulled into the parking lot below MI6 headquarters, parked, and headed upstairs. As it was, they stumbled on to Jonas, ripping into somebody in the hallway. As he turned and saw them, Jonas's glare widened to encompass the two of them. "What the hell is going on here?" he roared.

Wallace's eyebrows shot up. "I'm not sure what this is and what you think we're up to, but we're trying to find Amy."

"Where is she?" Jonas asked.

Wallace shook his head. "It appears she's been kidnapped. We're not sure whether you guys had a hand in it or that was just a coincidence."

From the look of complete shock on Jonas's face, it was obvious that he'd never once considered such a thing.

At that, Wallace nodded. "I'm really glad to see it wasn't you."

"What the hell are you talking about?" Jonas roared.

"Thinking of the job she was brought in to do," he explained, "we couldn't help but wonder if somebody in your office decided some test was in order."

Jonas blinked several times, and then he slowly sagged onto the closest wall. "Good God," he muttered, with a headshake. "That would be just beyond everything."

"Sure, but it's also not out of the realm of possibility," Riff declared. "And we all know it."

At that, Jonas shot him a hard look. "I sure didn't have anything to do with it."

"Maybe not, but that doesn't mean the British government didn't."

"No, it doesn't," he murmured, rubbing his hands through his hair. "Good Christ, I need to make some calls and see what I can come up with. You guys keep trying to find her." Then he turned to face Wallace. "If you know she's been kidnapped, where the hell is she? Did they ask for ransom? Is that what this is about?"

"No, as far as we're concerned, we're still looking at you guys," Riff interjected smoothly, not letting Jonas off the hook. "Other than that, we don't know where she is. For now we're presuming London."

Jonas looked confused for a moment. "So how do you

know she didn't just walk away? Decided the job wasn't for her and just packed up and left?"

"I'm sure plenty of people may wonder if she did exactly that, particularly if she'd been picked up as some MI6 test. If she fails, what's to stop somebody from just deep-sixing her?"

At that, Jonas swore again. "We're a government agency here, not the mafia."

"Not all that easy to tell the difference sometimes," Riff noted, with a wry grin directed at Wallace, apparently unable to avoid pushing Jonas's buttons at every turn. "Also Terk's been in contact with her."

Wallace frowned at his partner, trying to slow down Riff's attacks on Jonas.

Riff shrugged back at Wallace. "I'm still not convinced that one of Jonas's bosses isn't involved in this. Governments being what they are and all," he added, with a hard look at Jonas.

"I know you've got this problem with governments in general because of your *own* government," Jonas pointed out, "and trust me that I wouldn't have brought you in on this, except that obviously something's happened." He shook his head. "Typical that you would turn it around and make it sound like it was me." And, with that, he stormed off, leaving the two men standing here, staring at each other.

"I don't think Amy's disappearance has anything to do with Jonas," Wallace noted.

"No, unfortunately I don't either." Riff turned to Wallace. "Didn't you say you had some directional kinds of abilities?"

"Yeah, I do—to a certain extent—but nothing like we need here."

"What do you mean, nothing like this? She's missing. So

can't you just pinpoint where she is?"

"Of course not," Wallace replied, as he groaned. "She's been gone too long for us to track her by the energy left at the hotel. It's dissipated already. Short of your hacking into MI6's surveillance tapes, we're still waiting for the CCTV cameras. I don't understand what's taking so long."

Just then Riff's phone rang. He looked down at the screen and answered it. "Terk, what's up?" he asked. "Did you guys get anywhere on the cameras?"

"No, of course not."

Riff listened in a little bit longer and nodded. "I just braced Jonas about it, and, as far as I'm concerned, he could easily be involved in this. … Yeah, I know. I know that you don't seem to think so. That doesn't mean I'll believe you just because you say so." He groaned and listened to Terk for a moment. "I know. I know. Fine." When he ended the call, he turned and glared at Wallace. "What would you do for MI6 if you came on board here?"

"They were looking at me running the team," he shared, with a shrug.

Riff stared at him. "Does that mean you have skills equal to what Terk has?"

"Nope, sure don't," he admitted. "I don't think *we* even know what Terk has for skills, much less MI6, which is one of their main problems. They're fishing for anything they can get their hands on, but I don't know what they're really looking for."

Riff snorted. "*That* I can believe. I can't figure out why they didn't go to the source in the first place. No offense."

"I think Terk probably turned him down, not trusting governments in general anymore."

At that, Riff nodded. "That would make total sense, but

it still doesn't make any sense to bring in somebody green."

"I didn't say I was green," Wallace corrected in exasperation. "I just don't have the same level of skill that Terk does."

"So, what do you do?" Riff asked.

"I'm a precog and can see … some things in the dark. Unfortunately I can't control it."

"Of course not. That's the problem with precogs. Don't mind me, but I think they're fairly useless." Riff turned and headed out of the MI6 building.

Following quickly behind, Wallace asked, "Where are you going?" And then quickly changed his question to, "Where are *we* going?"

Riff glanced at him and shrugged. "Unless you're a precog who can come up with any answers as to where Amy is, I suggest we do it the old-fashioned way."

Wallace followed him back to the rig. "Why is it I feel as if you're not telling me something?"

Riff shrugged. "I do well at finding things," he muttered, "gathering intel. So I'll need my laptop, which is in the rig. I'll access some MI6 secret files myself. It would have been much more fun to use Jonas's own equipment to infiltrate their system, but I figure I've pricked his ego enough today. Also, lately I've been a little off my game in some ways. It's a personal problem," he muttered. "Unfortunately we are creatures of moods and emotions, and, when things went wrong, … well, it set back a lot of my world."

"That's all very cryptic."

They got into the loaner MI6 rig and both reached for their laptops. As Wallace opened his up, he checked for any messages, but there was none. "If MI6 isn't playing some game themselves, … then somebody else is likely playing it for them." He wondered about the options. "Or it could be that somebody was serious about wanting to utilize Amy's skills, in which case they won't know if she has any, not unless she puts them to good use. And they will likely have to force her to show them."

"Which makes sense," Riff agreed, turning to look at him sideways. "But you know that it won't be good for her."

"No, it won't," Wallace admitted grimly. "The only way they'll force her to do something is if they put extreme pressure on her."

"And presumably she has a pretty high tolerance to resist their attempts."

"I don't know about that, especially since she's been very sick recently," Wallace shared. "As in very sick. She wouldn't give me the details, but she was obviously still under the weather slightly when she arrived here."

"That's not good," Riff said, "particularly if it's affected her abilities."

"It definitely has. Terk mentioned that too this morning. Amy's not even really sure what she can do."

"Which is even worse because she'll make good testing material."

"Or she'll make *great* testing material since she'll be exploring what she can do herself."

"Right, but that's not something any of us want her to go through with these unknown third parties involved," Riff muttered. "Assholes like this really won't care how things work. They'll just want to confirm that they get the results they want when they want it."

"Regardless of what it does to her, I presume."

Riff nodded. Still sitting in their parked vehicle, but, with his laptop open, Riff pointed at Wallace's laptop.

"While I peek into MI6's dark corners, why don't you check the street cams again, this time for service vehicles around the hotel at 11:15 p.m. last night, or Ubers, or the like?" Wallace nodded, as Riff began his online search.

Riff hacked into MI6's protected files, some employment related, some ops related, some about this new psychic team. Then he jumped on the dark web, searching for Psychics Wanted ads and such. He even telepathically asked Terk if he had heard rumblings of anybody wanting psychics really badly. Even that ended in a dead end for the moment.

An hour later Riff sat back in frustration and exclaimed, "How is that possible?"

Wallace groaned. "You had no luck either? I didn't see any service trucks until early this morning, like a bread delivery or whatnot. Either nothing suspicious went by the cams or the kidnappers rigged the cameras."

"Or," Riff suggested, frowning at Wallace, "the kidnappers already have a team with people who can do this energy shit. Maybe some energy worker did something to the cameras or knows how to set up a camouflage."

"Oh no. That would be our worst nightmare, so I'm not going there."

Riff glared at him. "We have occasionally come across people with these kinds of abilities who operate outside of the law. … It's never a good deal for anybody. And it doesn't give us much to go on, if that's what's happened here."

Wallace frowned. "What if she's still in the hotel?"

Riff stared at him in surprise. "What do you mean?"

"What if she didn't leave—because we didn't see a vehicle—and what if she's still there somewhere? An awful lot of rooms are in hotels, and some are in places most people don't even know about, like down in the basement or in the laundry area. Somewhere secluded, and who knows? Maybe it's connected to those underground tunnels that Levi and his team already alerted me to," he added. "They are sending me a tunnel map soon."

At that, Riff started to nod very slowly. "You could be right. A lot of service tunnels are under most of London," he muttered. "Hell, there's a whole city down there."

Wallace nodded. "Exactly. What if somebody figured it would be a whole lot easier just to keep Amy down there?"

Riff suggested, "If they didn't need to move her, that would be perfect. What we need then is to see where she could have gotten to, where the hotel elevator goes. Does it drop into the tunnels?"

"Hang on a minute. I got a new email." Wallace checked and found one from Levi's team, attaching subterranean blueprints, plus the blueprints for the hotel building itself. A moment later he opened them and smiled. He pointed to one of them. "This hotel was built on top of an old building foundation, with tunnels running right below it all."

"Yeah, they always do that here," Riff noted. "As long as it's structurally sound, they just bring down the old building and put the new building on top of the existing foundation. It's too much work to dig it up, especially if they should be unlucky enough to hit an old burial site or something. That puts a halt to construction for a long time. So they often just go down as far as they need to and build back up again."

Wallace looked over the blueprints and nodded slowly. "Plus, they avoid damaging the tunnels not too far below all that. I see sewer connections nearby Amy's hotel too."

Riff smiled. "So, it looks as if we're going sewer hunting." He looked over at him. "We'll need some gear."

Wallace looked up a store nearby that would give them

headlamps, flashlights, and better footwear. By the time they were decked out and heading underground toward the location they had chosen, Wallace noted that four hours had gone by. "That took way too long," he fretted.

"But we're now geared up and on our way," Riff stated.

Wallace muttered, "Ask Terk to send out a telepathic message to Amy, if he can. Or you do it. I can't seem to reach her. Tell Amy that we're on the way, and we'll get there as soon as we can." With that, Wallace still sent off his own message mentally, still hoping that maybe the energy field, that sense of communication coming, would open up her senses and would give her some reassurance that help was on the way.

Accessing the sewer system where they wouldn't be noticed, Wallace and Riff navigated their way toward their target location and soon came up into some of the big service tunnels underneath the hotel. With their flashlights and headlamps on, Wallace realized that this underground ecosystem was not only big enough to house a massive hotel itself but, at this moment, it seemed big enough to house half the city. He stared at Riff. "It's bigger than I imagined down here. How will we ever find her?"

Riff grinned. "Hopefully down here I'll do more of my specialty. Follow me."

And Riff led the way deeper into the tunnels.

CHAPTER 2

A MY WOKE, STOOD up slowly, and walked around, flapping her arms against the chill. She had no idea where she was, but, so far, the group had been friendly, coming in and out at regular intervals, bringing her food, tea, coffee, blankets, and seemingly whatever she needed. What she wasn't getting was answers or a visit from the people who were supposedly on their way to explain why she was here.

That part, above all else, really bothered her because now she was wondering whether anybody at all was coming or this was something completely different than all the scenarios going through her head. But, hey, she was prepared to do whatever she needed to do to get the hell out of here. When the door opened again, the same guard walked in, holding a cup of coffee.

He noted in an undertone, "Sorry it's so cold in here. We're having problems with the heat."

She nodded. "It's definitely cold, and it's clammy," she added, "as if we're underground. No windows are here."

"No, not in this room," he replied. "Something to do with the way the bylaws were written, with only so many bedrooms allowed. Since a room can't be called a bedroom unless it's got a window in it, building rooms without windows became a popular way to get around the rule."

It seemed to be a complete BS story to her, but, then

again, when it came to city codes, she didn't know much. She just nodded and accepted the cup. "How much longer?" she asked.

"Hopefully, not very long at all," he stated cheerfully, and, with that, he turned and walked back out.

She stared at the door suspiciously, wondering if she really was a prisoner. They hadn't come outright and said she was, but it had been implied from the start. She sipped her coffee as she stared at the door. If this was a test, she was certain she'd failed, and that was good. She didn't want anything to do with a group that would do this to her. Whatever was going on here was just wrong. She figured, at some point, either they were afraid she would figure it out herself or they were waiting for her to use her energy skills.

That's the part that really worried her. She wasn't exactly sure what she could do. She hadn't lied when she had told Terk that everything was changing, since everything had changed. Plus, if she were underground—as she suspected she was—she was surrounded by thick concrete walls, which definitely hindered telepathy and other energy skills. Her abilities, which had always been similar to a locator, wouldn't help if she were the lost one.

As she considered her guard's words, she realized he hadn't specifically denied that they were underground. He hadn't really told her anything. As a matter of fact, once she thought about it, she realized his answers had been more evasive than anything else.

Frowning at that, she walked over to the door and turned the knob. The knob turned under her hand, but the door didn't budge when she went to pull on it. She stepped back and glared at the door. "That answers that question." She stared at the room around her. "Can't say I appreciate being a prisoner."

Knowing that they were probably listening in and laughing at her, she walked back over and sat down on the bed, pulling her knees up against her chest, wondering just what the hell was going on. She thought she heard a whisper, something subtle and faint, but something was definitely there. She closed her eyes and called out to the ethers. She couldn't quite grasp who or what it was.

She called out for Terk, and he came online immediately. The reception was staticky, clarity coming in and out.

We have people looking for you, he told her. *Have you learned anything useful? Anything about these people?*

No, just that they're still waiting for someone, and I am still a prisoner.

You know for sure you're a prisoner? he asked, his tone sharp.

At least that was her interpretation of the fading energy. *Yes, I tried to open the door but no luck.*

That's what we expected anyway, he replied.

Yeah, maybe you did, but I didn't, she snapped. *I was still thinking that this was some test, whether MI6 or private.*

I'm not sure it isn't, he noted. *It could very well be that they're checking to see if you do have any abilities and what it'll take for you to use them to get out of there.*

Which is BS, she snapped. *No way I would use my abilities in this situation.*

Why not? he asked curiously.

Because, if they found out, if they got any confirmation that I am an energy worker, then, chances are, … they would never let me go.

Terk agreed. *That's a good point, and I'm glad you realize it. They probably won't release you anyway.*

She sucked back her breath. *You didn't have to say that.*

Right, and yet I don't really believe in couching the truth. You and I both know that this is a serious scenario, and we're doing everything we can to find you, but that doesn't mean it'll happen soon enough.

She winced, trying to keep her expression calm in case she was being watched. She didn't want anyone to know what she was doing in her head. *If they're expecting me to do something, but I'm not, do you think they'll up the ante?*

A long moment of silence came from Terk, and then he whispered, *I'm afraid so.*

When would that likely happen? she asked, striving for calm, but inside she felt the chills rattling through her soul.

I don't know how long they'll give you. That'll be up to them. Chances are, they won't have too much patience. Someone has told them that you can do something, and they'll be all over finding out what that is, how you do it, and what triggers are effective, he shared in a sympathetic tone. *Unfortunately the process of getting to those answers, or the methods they are likely to utilize to get you to show them, won't be fun.* Giving her these nuggets of wisdom, he was gone.

She sat here pondering what he'd shared, when the door opened again, and the man she'd seen earlier stepped inside and glaring at her. She looked at him blandly. "Hi. Back again so soon? Did you find whoever is waiting to see me?"

He shook his head, looked around the room, then crossed his arms and leaned against the wall.

"Problem?" she asked curiously.

"You seem to be relatively calm."

"I wouldn't say calm," she clarified. "It does appear that I'm your prisoner, which isn't something that'll make anybody happy."

He smirked. "You tried the door, did you?"

"You know I did," she stated. "Obviously you're watching me, though I'm not sure how or why, but it's pretty gross. But, hey, apparently you guys are into that stuff."

Immediately the smile fell off his face, but he continued to glare at her. "Don't even start with me on that shit," he spat. "That's not who we are."

"How do I know? You haven't told me who you are, what you are, or anything else," she declared. "So you can say anything you want, and it won't mean shit to me. I'm working off your actions, not your words."

He stared at her and turned around to walk away.

"You could just tell me what this is all about," she added, striving for a conversational voice. But seeing the smirk on his face, she realized she'd failed. Even though it was the hardest thing to do, she shrugged. "Whatever." And, with that, she leaned against the wall and relaxed on the bed.

He stopped midstep and looked at her curiously. "How come you're not worried?"

"Not worried about what?" she asked, rolling her head toward him. "About what you're doing? So far you haven't told me anything, but, if this is a kidnapping, and you're after a ransom, you'll be out of luck because I don't have any money," she explained. "Nobody's speaking the truth here, so I'm not sure you guys even know what you want with me. But somebody went to great lengths to kidnap me out of my hotel, so it must be important."

"Are you sure that's what happened?" he asked, his eyes opening wide. "I don't think so. I'm pretty sure you came to us."

"That's definitely not the truth," she replied. "I don't even know why you would attempt to lie over something as simple to refute as that."

His gaze narrowed. "You're pretty cocky, aren't you?"

"Absolutely not," she countered. "I'm just starting to get a little pissed because I'm sitting here in the cold, in the dark, underground, wondering what you guys are up to. I don't know when you'll decide this isn't worth your time and let me go."

"*What* isn't worth our time?" he pounced.

"I have no idea," she admitted, staring at him with a flat expression. "You keep telling me that somebody wants to see me, but I'm not sure whether somebody wants to see me or you're just sitting there, like voyeurs, always watching me. Honestly, I find that a little disturbing. By the way, I need to go to the bathroom again. I'm grateful for the washroom here, but, if you've got cameras in there too, well, gee, you're about to miss out on the show that's about to come up," she said sarcastically.

He flushed a dull red and glared at her.

She smiled and asked, "What's the matter? You don't like being called a predator, when you are watching me? You don't like anything I have to say about that? Is that not what you expected?"

He stiffened, then turned and walked out, slamming the door behind him.

She smirked, got up, then used the bathroom because, well, who knew what would happen now. They might come take her out of the room after that little scenario.

She probably shouldn't have pushed it, but she could only do so much when it came to these assholes. She now realized that this wouldn't get any better. It would just be a case of more pain for her, until they finally showed their hand. Unfortunately she was pretty sure that Terk might be right—she was a test subject to see what she could do.

If she didn't do anything, they would up the ante. Then she would end up in a worse scenario than she had been. Yet, as they made it more uncomfortable for her, looking to see if she would try to escape, they just might reveal their hand in the process. Why they would think she had any abilities, she didn't know, but it all came back to the job interview she'd been foolish enough to come to England for.

It even sounded stupid to say that it was a job interview, since it wasn't really. Yet she'd come over to talk to them about this new department. One of the things that she wanted to know was why they weren't talking to Terk. He was the guy who had managed the previous department for the US. So, if MI6 wanted to set up something like that here, surely you would want the best guy on their team, and that would undoubtedly be Terk.

Amy frowned. But if it wasn't Jonas's hand to deal, then maybe he really didn't have a choice in the matter. Sometimes working with governments was way more convoluted than necessary. She laughed at that because it wasn't just *sometimes*. It was all the time. As everybody did their own checks and balances to cover their own butts, it ended up just making it worse instead of better.

She was pretty darn sure that was exactly what was happening right now. She would sort it out with them when she got out of here, but somebody had found out about her through that request for her appearance at that meeting. Betrayal was something she found very hard to deal with. Somebody in the government had betrayed somebody else in the government—no surprise there.

She shook her head and laughed again, then settled back, determined not to let them get to her. She just didn't know how long this would last and how ugly it could get, before they decided she was way too comfortable. Then they would make it way the hell worse for her.

She closed her eyes and tried to rest. When she opened her eyes again, she realized she'd fallen asleep. The door was opening ever-so-slightly, and she stiffened, watching, but instead of her captor stepping inside, something was dropped in. She scrunched up to the back of the bed as a large snake slithered toward her. She sucked in her breath and stared at it. "If that isn't a confirmation, I don't know what is," she muttered out loud.

No answer came from anybody, but she knew for sure that she was being watched now. Somebody wanted to see what she would do with this. As much as she didn't particularly like snakes, she knew this guy was also terrified by whatever circumstance he'd just found himself in. As she watched, it slithered around, looking for a way out too, and she smiled.

"You find a way out, buddy, and then I'll follow."

Of course, she would need a hell of a lot bigger space to accommodate her than him. As she watched, he went all the way around the room. Now, as it got closer to her, it clearly smelled her scent and realized she was here. She had no idea whether or not he was dangerous, but any animal in this circumstance was dangerous, and it didn't matter whether they were considered lethal or not.

Every animal would fight to defend itself, and this poor critter had already been captured. Kind of like her. It was probably a good bet on their part that she would not take kindly to a snake, but she found very few in the animal world distressing enough to really upset her. Mostly the two-legged predators offended her. Which meant that this guy, as long as he didn't bite her, was totally okay with her. Drawn to her body heat, he slithered up onto the bed. She stiffened as he got closer and closer.

"It's cold in here, isn't it?" she asked him in a conversational tone. "It's all right. It's all right. I'm not going to hurt you."

He wasn't showing any signs of aggression or attack. He just appeared to be looking for warmth.

"I wonder what they did to you, poor thing," she murmured, then realized how it would look to these guys if they were watching her, expecting her to freak out while dealing with a snake perched on her bed. That was hardly much of a test, but she was afraid that now the tests would start in earnest, whether she liked them or not.

She looked down at the snake, sliding closer and closer to her leg, before it slowly crept up against her body and wrapped itself up underneath her knee, soaking up as much of her heat as it could. "You and me both, buddy, you and me both."

She settled back to wait for their next move because this one had just sided with her, and nothing much they could do about it.

WALLACE FOLLOWED BEHIND Riff in the darkness, their flashlights and headlamps bouncing across concrete tunnel walls, revealing water dripping down and occasionally rats scrambling away from them.

When they came up to a series of stairs, Riff asked him, "You picking up anything?"

He nodded. "Definitely, I just don't know what," he

muttered. "Everything is muffled down here."

"That's because you're looking for some direct response," Riff pointed out. "Don't just absorb the atmosphere. Recognize this setting for what it is, and note that it won't interfere in any way with any signal you're getting—because your signals aren't traveling the normal way of other signals. That's your brain kicking in, trying to use logic. Use only your psychic senses instead, and don't allow anything else to get in the way of it."

Wallace understood in theory what Riff was saying, and it did make sense because the mind did tend to kick in and say, *Oh, you're underground, so no signal.* Yet telepathy was not the type of signals they were sending, and they didn't need to be aboveground to send them.

Wallace kept sending off a locator beacon signal, directing it to find Amy, trying to let her know that he was coming. He was hoping that something as simple as that would give almost a metronome effect, and she would pick it up on the airwaves. He sent it out, knowing that it would also reverberate within the tunnels and should amplify itself, without his having to put out too much energy on it. As they moved up the stairs, they found themselves at a crossroads, with another structure, another tunnel, cutting off in a different direction.

Riff walked past it, but Wallace couldn't. He called out, "I need to go down there."

Riff turned, stared at him, and came back in his direction. "You sure?"

Wallace nodded. "Yeah, I'm sure. I don't know what's down here, but I need to go." He added in a clipped note, "You can go on that way."

"I think we need to stay together."

Wallace hesitated, then shook his head. "I don't know that we have time."

Swearing, Riff nodded. "Fine, I'll head up this way then. You keep going that way, but stay in communication." And, with that, Riff was gone.

Unable to ignore this pressure inside that screamed at Wallace to move faster, he raced down this new tunnel toward whatever lay at the other end, just wishing he could see something, anything, that would give him a clue.

As he got farther along, he heard a voice. He hesitated and crept closer, finding a man on the ground. Wallace wasn't sure if he was homeless, but he looked to be in a bad way. Wallace crouched beside him. "Hey, what's up?"

The guy gasped. "I need help, man, I need help."

"I can call you some help." Wallace pulled out his phone, swearing as he checked the bars because, of course, no signals were down here. He decided to use telepathy, only he had no idea if he could reach Riff. His telepathy only seemed to work with Amy.

The guy kept trying to breathe through his pain. So when he spoke next, it was around his breathing. "Phones don't work down here, ... but I've been calling out for hours. ... Those assholes did this."

Wallace's heart stilled. "What assholes?"

"Some guys." He gasped for more air. "I don't know who they are." He groaned. "I was kidnapped and held captive for a couple days. Then they wanted me to do some shit for them, and I just ... I couldn't do it and didn't know what they were talking about. They thought I was some other dude, ... but I wasn't. I was in the wrong place at the wrong time." He gave a sarcastic laugh that set off a fit of coughing. "That's the story of my life."

It was easy for Wallace to see the man was in bad shape. Bending, he slipped his arms under the man's body. "Okay, take a deep breath." And, with that, he straightened up.

The broken man screamed in pain.

"Did they beat you?"

The man nodded. "One of them didn't like me. Every time I opened my mouth, he pretty well smacked it closed," he murmured. "Then, as I failed to do what they wanted, the beatings got worse."

As he carried the man back toward Riff, Wallace added, "Tell me what happened."

"I was in a hotel downtown," he began, between groans. "I came to London for a job interview, went to the pub, and was talking to some guys there because I felt good about the interview. One of the guys asked me if my name was Wallace, and I replied, yeah, though I didn't know how the hell he knew."

At the name, Wallace himself stiffened. "Your name is Wallace?" he asked incredulously.

"Yeah, Gerry Wallace," he stated.

"Ah."

"My name set him off," Gerry muttered.

As Wallace took another step, it jarred Gerry, who cried out in pain. "Anything broken?"

"I don't know, likely though," he muttered. "They left me in here to die. I'm sure of that. I'm just not the dying kind."

As Wallace got out to the other tunnel, Riff waited at the T intersection. He took one look at the man and frowned. "What the hell?"

"Hardly what we came for, I know, but, more important, he has information, and I think he was already kidnapped by the same guys." Then he quickly explained what the guy had told him. Riff stared at his partner. "So, you're also a target then."

"Yeah, makes me wonder what the fuck they're up to with her."

The injured man stared at him. "What do you mean, you're a target?"

"My name is Wallace," he explained. "I also came into town for an interview. Hardly a job interview, but it was to lead a team for the British government, so I was over here for talks about it. A woman who was to be part of the whole deal has also been kidnapped, and we're down here trying to find her."

"Shit, man," the guy muttered. "Good thing you're the one who rescued me."

"Did they say anything about a woman?"

"Yeah, they did. That they had to pick her up, but she wouldn't present much of a challenge. They were hoping that she did a better job than I did."

"What did they ask you to do?" Wallace asked urgently.

"Jesus, just strange stuff that I don't even know about. I really don't know what they expected, but they kept getting angry with me because I couldn't do anything. I kept telling them that I would do whatever they wanted, but they had to tell me what they wanted me to do. One did say something about being a show pony, but that's … I don't even know what the hell he meant by that."

"Did they mention psychics or anything weird like that?"

"Yeah, he told me to bend spoons or do something like that, but what the hell? Who can bend spoons?" he cried out. And even that much movement caused him to cry out in pain.

"Okay, take it easy."

Riff stepped up to ask him, "Do you have any idea where they kept you?"

"All I know is that I got out of the tunnel, and I can't walk," he shared. "Both my legs are damaged, so they carried me for a while, and dropped me where this guy found me. So it's got to be somewhere nearby."

Riff nodded. "You go look," he suggested to Wallace. "I'll get some help for this guy." And, with that, Riff snatched the injured man and took off.

Wallace turned, stared down the tunnel where he'd come from, then swore and sent out a message in his head. *I'm coming, kiddo. I'm coming.*

And dammit, for the first time, he almost got this faint acknowledgment, almost Amy's voice, saying, *Hurry it up please.*

CHAPTER 3

A MY SHIFTED UNEASILY in the new room, set up as a meeting area with no bed this time. She took a measure of her surroundings. Five men were here, but four men stood farther back, not close enough to be threatening. She sat at a table, with the fifth man seated across from her. He seemed smug but not the leader of this group. The angry burly man off to the side appeared to be in charge. She looked over at him and gave him a tentative smile, probably ruffling his feathers that she had singled him out. She wasn't exactly sure what was going on, but she heard something rattling around in the background. She thought she'd heard Wallace, but that made no sense—and was hours ago. Since then there had been nothing.

When the smug man across the table held out his hand, she placed hers atop his, wondering what game they were playing at. He held her hand for a moment, his eyes closed, then looked over at the other men and nodded.

"So, what did I just do?" she asked. "Win a car?"

He snorted. "No, but I can read people's thoughts."

"No," she countered. "You might *intuit* people's thoughts, but you can't read them. *Reading* would imply something visual to see."

His gaze narrowed. "What I can *read* is the name *Wallace*."

"That doesn't take any mind-reading, just some spying, and we know you guys are watchers," she stated, taking another dig at the group. "Wallace was at the meeting with me."

He nodded. "But you were just thinking about him."

"Why wouldn't I?" she asked curiously. "One of you guys mentioned something about missing him. So now it's constantly in the back of my mind that you could be trying to trap him into whatever this craziness is that you've got going on here."

He gave her a ghost of a smile.

She gave him a bland look in return, doing everything she could to increase the buildup of her defenses.

"And even now," he added, "you're trying to block me."

"If you could possibly read my mind, why wouldn't I be blocking you? Do these guys let you *read their minds* too?" One of the guys on the far side shifted uneasily. "If you can read my mind, then no reason you can't read theirs."

She wasn't sure that she should be poking the proverbial bears in this room, but anything to distract the grandiose guy from her mind, while she threw up even more defenses, seemed to be a good idea. Plus, she was sowing doubt into the minds of his buddies. For some reason, it had never occurred to her that they might have some psychic, fake or real, on their team.

Then she gave a half laugh. "Besides, if *you* can do all that, what the hell do you guys need me for?" She turned and looked at the others, frowning. Then refocused on the guy at the table with her. "Unless they don't think you're the real thing. Otherwise, I don't understand what's going on here."

"You don't understand because we haven't told you anything," stated the angry burly man, who had been shifting uneasily on the far side.

Since he felt free to speak up, she had another reason to peg him as the leader of this group.

He glared at her with a hint of fury that he masked very quickly. "I don't like anything about this."

"Ah." Amy nodded in understanding. "You're very much the kind of person who likes to see and hear things for yourself then. It's difficult to believe all this nebulous woo-woo stuff, isn't it?"

He gave a clipped nod. "It sounds too much like fakes, charlatans, and total BS to me," he stated bluntly.

"I agree," she said, with a murmur. "I was quite surprised that MI6 was looking at doing something like that, but, of course, they're just building on an old CIA program done during the Second World War. But then again, Russia had also been doing the same thing, so not much difference here."

The three minions leaned forward, remaining silent—until now. One frowned, asking, "Seriously?"

She nodded. "Yes, quite a bit of research is online. They would have somebody sit in a room and mentally place themselves in these other buildings across the world—all to get an idea of what people were up against, what was happening to prisoners, thinking they could see things that would help them win the war," she shared. "I don't think we'll ever find the actual data on paper that gave the true results as they came about. Much more likely, the papers they released are highly cleansed versions that they think the public can handle. Because, if you can believe in all that, then what's stopping us from believing in UFOs?"

One of the minions in the back laughed and admitted,

"I definitely believe in UFOs."

The burly man glared at him and snapped, "Shut up." The head guy returned his gaze to her. "If MI6 is doing a program like this, and you were brought in, then you must have some ability."

"MI6 is basing that on some things that happened to me when I was a child," she explained. "I woke up from a car accident, speaking about all kinds of stuff. ... For a while afterward I did have abilities, things that I could do."

"Like?"

"I could look at you and say, *Hey, you're wearing white underwear*, or *He's wearing blue underwear*, or whatever," she shared, with a laugh. "And it went on until I hit puberty. Then, ... man, it all changed," she said, with a shrug. "Yeah, it was fun while it lasted, but it's not as if it was useful at all."

All the men stilled as they contemplated that information.

Burly noted, "There's no record of you having an accident."

She stared at him. "Wow, so you checked out my history, but you didn't do a deep dive into my background?" she asked lightly. "Or you were just checking out my recent history as it pertained to England and the US? When all this happened, I was a child, living in Brazil, where my father was working at the university at the time," she shared. "I'm sure if you checked that history, or at least took your search in that direction, you would find that several newspaper articles were published back then. My parents tried to squash as much of it as they could, not wanting it to become an unhealthy obsession," she murmured.

Some of the men nodded.

The man across from her announced, "My name is

Dominic, by the way."

She looked over at him and nodded. "Thanks, Dom."

His eyebrows shot up. "How do you know people call me Dom?"

"It's hardly a paranormal thing," she stated in exasperation. "Almost nobody will let that mouthful out all the time. *Dominic* is just way too long, so it's bound to get shortened to *Dom*." She shrugged. "That's what people do, and it's not psychic. More about common sense."

He sat back and stared at her. "We've tested several other people in here before," he murmured. "It didn't go so well for them when they didn't agree to the testing."

"I haven't been asked about any testing," she pointed out, staring at him. "By the way, what do you mean, *it didn't go well for them?*"

From the back corner, the burly man snapped, "That's enough. She doesn't need to know anything."

Dom nodded. "I guess I was looking for some reaction, something empathetic, something …"

"Like fear?" she interrupted. "That's what you want, right? You want me afraid. You want me terrified of what you'll do to me, so that I start spitting out whatever it is you want to hear. The problem with that technique is that people then spit out information in the hopes that it's what you want to hear, but it's not the truth. It's them just trying to survive. It's them trying to save their sorry ass in order to not die or whatever it is they think you'll do to them. Is that what you want? You want people to start making up things in order to get you some answers that will hopefully make you stop this madness and leave them alone?" She looked around the room, directing her gaze at each one.

The burly man glared at her.

She nodded. "I didn't think so. Surely whatever reason you have for getting me here is because you want the truth, whatever that means. If I can't help you, I can't help you. If I can, then I can. It really is as simple as that."

"It's not that simple," Dom declared. "People think they know something, but, in truth, they don't."

"They'll know *something*," she argued, staring at him sharply, "but it'll mean something to them, not necessarily to you. If I look at you and tell you something about your life, it's only because of whatever symbolism I see. It doesn't mean that I'm reaching into your mind and that I can see you and the folder that states, *ten years ago, you did this, this, and this*," she said. "I'll see an image, like a water cooler, and it's telling me that your life is running away because that tap is broken, and the water is just filtering away rather quickly," she explained, trying to describe the images that were in her head right now.

She continued. "That's what *I* see, but that water cooler won't mean anything to you. If you can relate to the fact that the water is running away and that your life is running away, yet you have no control because it's broken, then maybe you would understand what I meant. Otherwise, it won't mean anything to you. So, it'll sound false or made up, when in fact it's not because it's exactly what I see and how I interpret the information, versus what you know and receive."

The burly guy walked several steps forward and looked at Dom. "Is that correct?"

Dom settled back in a negligent and almost arrogant manner, but he nodded. "To some extent, yes. A lot of people do not get statements or actual words, they get images. They get pictures of things that have a symbolism to them. She's right. That symbolism isn't something that anybody would necessarily relate to but her." Dom gave her a grin. "Which, in fact, supports the idea that we probably are talking to the right person."

"You haven't *found* anything. You've somehow learned that I was at a meeting with MI6," she pointed out. "And you also know that they dropped me off at my hotel, which is where you kidnapped me. However, if that MI6 meeting had been deemed top secret or of any importance, I would never have been allowed to return to the hotel."

At that, the burly man stiffened again and nodded. "I did consider that," he muttered. "It's not good news that you were released, and the other man wasn't."

"Wallace, you mean," she clarified. "That's quite true. … I felt very much as if I had just failed the interview," she muttered, but then she shrugged. "They didn't even tell us what we were there for, outside of the fact that they're trying to put together a team. But they're always putting together teams, but the kinds of teams, the testing, and the work those teams will do, that's an entirely different story."

Burly asked, "What did they say? Tell us exactly what you were told."

She pondered that for a moment, and then, with her hands out in front of her, she ticked off the items. "The job would start in about a month. I would have to relocate to England. The work would be top secret, so I would have to pass all their clearance testing before I could be allowed in. They didn't give me very much in the way of details, something about extrasensory perception work. Of course I would have to pass certain proficiency tests in order to get in." She shrugged. "The range of pay was lovely, at least three times what I'm currently making, but they also told me, more or less, that I couldn't talk about my job to anybody, including family, friends, or loved ones, and that I wouldn't have any personal life for at least three years, while they worked to develop this."

At that, the men just stared at her silently, as if processing what she'd shared, but not really understanding if it was of any value.

"And because they dropped me off at the hotel and kept Wallace, who I thought was staying at the same hotel as well, I assumed I didn't make the first cut," she shared. "I am female after all, and we're well aware of the fact that women tend to get hired way less than men. So, if Wallace was the stronger candidate, then it makes sense that, out of the two of us, he would be the one to be hired."

Dom smiled. "I have met more male psychics than females. I've met more female charlatan psychics."

"Sure," she conceded, "the tarot readers in the carnival tents, where people come in, pay five bucks, and want to be told that they'll meet a tall, dark, and handsome person tomorrow," she noted. "That's a very different story than what MI6 was talking about."

"How do you know that?" Burly asked. "I thought they didn't really give you an idea."

"No, but they told me that they were setting up a government-sanctioned program. So, we're not talking colorful turbans and dark tents and big fancy rings on my fingers," she said, with a laugh. She shook her head. "But I really don't know who, what, where, how, or why this plan matters to you, and I don't understand why you care," she declared, bewildered. "Unless you're trying to set up your own group."

"That's what we're trying to do," Dom admitted, smiling at her. "But, in order to do that, we have to find people who have abilities."

"Most people with abilities hide them," she stated, with a shrug.

"Why is that?" one of the minions behind her asked.

She turned to look at them and realized that two of the men behind her looked similar, maybe not brothers but potentially related. "Because of things like this," she said, waving her arm around the room. "You wouldn't give a crap about me if you didn't know that I had gone to that interview. And, having gone to that interview, you're immediately wondering what I know, what I can do, and trying to figure out whether I would work for whatever it is you want," she offered. "But anybody who has abilities, either they use them as entertaining tricks at college dorm parties," she added, with a sneer, "or they keep to themselves. And, of course, you have those who work with the police."

"You don't work with the police," Dom pointed out, leaning forward. "Why not?"

"Remember that time period when I still had all those abilities? I did work with the police back then," she clarified, "and it was brutal. I was dealing with rapists and child murderers and missing children," she shared, even now the tears catching in the back of her throat. "When I hit puberty, and I lost that ability, it was such a relief to not have to deal with that dark side anymore. I was just grateful."

"So, you're saying you don't have those abilities anymore?" Burly asked.

"That's exactly what I'm saying," she murmured. "I have this faint bit of something, maybe 10 percent of what I used to have. ... It's not anything where I could go to the police and say, *Hey, I know where this missing kid is*, which is what I could and did do back then." She shrugged. "But then the hormones kicked in, and apparently my brain turned off, so here I am, not a teenager, and all this is just a shit show." She snorted at her half-assed joke.

Yet, as she stared around at her audience, and they stared back at her uncomprehendingly, she realized none of these guys knew about humor or had any understanding as to what she meant. She sighed. "So now that you know that, what else do you need to know?"

They looked at each other, and Burly motioned at Dom. "Take her back to her room. We need to talk this over."

Dom hopped up and said, "Let's go."

She got to her feet, and, with a quick glance at the others—who were all staring at Burly—she followed Dom back to her room. As she got inside, she turned to him. "I guess I said the wrong thing, didn't I?"

"If you told the truth, it's fine. If you lied, yeah, it won't go so well."

And, with that, he slammed the door in her face.

WALLACE KEPT WALKING underground in the sewers, trying to figure out where the hell he was going. He passed a couple people, asked them if they knew anything about rooms, dungeons, or places where a prisoner could be held, but they just stared at him and shuffled away silently.

He hadn't meant to upset them, but obviously it was a hard thing for anybody to deal with. That was not far from how he was feeling himself right about now. When he found another homeless man sitting at one of the entrances, he stopped and spoke to him for a few minutes. He was at least a little friendlier. He had already heard through what appeared to be an instant sewer grapevine about the other man called Wallace and his rescue. When the homeless man realized he was talking to the man who had been part of that rescue, he became friendlier.

"We're just trying to find a missing woman now," Wallace shared. "She's been kidnapped, and we believe she's being held down here somewhere because Wallace was kept down here."

"Don't that just figure," the man muttered, shaking his head and waving his hands. "This is a place for people to come and get away. We like the privacy we get down here."

Wallace pondered that. "Do you though? Is it that you really enjoy it down here, or is it more about getting away from all that up there? Do you all use this as a place to hide from the chaos up there?"

The other man stared at him for a long moment and nodded. "Good point." He gave him a half smile. "As far as the woman, I don't know of a place where they would have kept her, but some parts of this tunnel we consider haunted," he murmured. "You might want to check out those places."

"*Haunted* because you hear voices and see tracks and things like that?"

"Exactly." He nodded. "You're thinking that maybe it's your gal?"

"I'm wondering if it's the people who are holding her at least," Wallace clarified.

"An awful lot of old storage rooms down here could have been converted to holding rooms," he shared.

"Wallace told me that his room had no outside light, no windows, at least where he was kept."

"That could be it then," the man agreed, as he spat some chewing tobacco onto the slime all around them. "I don't know why anybody would want to use those spaces though.

It's a pretty rough place."

"If you're kidnapping people, *rough* becomes relative, you know?" Wallace noted. "Where would I find these places?"

At that, he was given directions deeper and farther into the maze. Taking his leave, he sent off a message on his phone, hoping it would transmit something to Riff eventually. He added a short telepathic message too. Still, it would be damn hard to keep up any communication down here. Yet he kept trudging along, picking up the pace, knowing that whatever was going on with Amy would be happening now, given the time frame from Gerry Wallace. The closer Wallace got, the more worried he became that it had taken far too long. The last thing he wanted was for them to hurt Amy, then dump her and run.

He felt an odd energy, almost … not shifty but unsettled, as if, indeed, ghosts were around the place. That was a little disturbing after what the homeless man had mentioned. Yet Wallace also knew that, if somebody was hanging around this place, those inside could very easily start rumors to keep people away.

If people heard an area was haunted, that would bring in seekers too, so Wallace doubted the homeless down here would encourage tourists, not if the homeless truly liked the respite this underworld provided. So maybe they kept the rumors to themselves to protect their privacy.

And, with that, Wallace picked up the pace, running now, using his flashlight and headlamp in a searching motion to stay on track. When he came to the next Y, he shifted direction and headed into what was even blacker and smellier, coated with an even slicker slime. As he ran another good one hundred feet in, he reached a bend and another break in the sewer line, with another line joining it.

As he approached, he found footprints coming into this line, so another entrance in and out was nearby. Taking a moment, he headed down the new tunnel, where the footprints had been coming from, and quickly found himself at an outside exit that could be a sewer pipe, draining into some sump pond.

It was just big enough for him to walk without any trouble. And that also worried him because what if somebody or something opened these drains and flooded the tunnels? Also, if someone was using these tunnels, did they have cameras installed? It was so dark he could barely see where he was going, let alone see cameras.

He would feel better if he knew for sure either way, but there really wasn't any time to sort it out. If he had to take a bath in sewage, it would not be the worst event of his life, but it would stick with him for a long time and likely make his top ten worst things list. Shaking that thought from his mind, he headed back down the way he'd come and followed the footsteps back onto the main line that he had been previously on. Looking carefully, he saw quite a few tracks, which meant it was heavily used, and people were even now active on this path, and that meant something completely different.

He needed to confirm he wasn't seen, and, if a guard was up ahead, Wallace's lights would be the first thing noticed. He took a quick look around to check that nothing unforeseen was in his immediate vicinity and quickly shut down his light and his lamp and doggedly headed on, going in deeper and deeper.

CHAPTER 4

SINCE THAT STRANGE meeting, Amy had had no other communication with the group. The new room where the meeting had been held and her locked room were just a short hallway apart. She still didn't know whether she was in some basement or further underground. She detected the overpowering smell of ground coffee, which always were stronger than the brewed version or the used grounds. She doubted it was to serve to their *guests* but to cover up the smells otherwise around here.

She'd had food brought in, just another simple sandwich and a bottle of water, but she was grateful. They had also removed the poor snake. She missed him. He'd been a companion, both of them caught in the same situation. She hoped they hadn't hurt him. As she sat here, huddling in the darkness, wondering at the dank cold around her, she heard a muffled sound, then what she envisioned as harsh jolts of movements outside her door. Then suddenly she had this inner sense that she was alone.

She didn't know why and didn't know how, but she felt a weird emptiness. She walked up to the door and called out, but she got no answer. She hadn't really tried to do that before, so she couldn't tell if silence now was a different response. As she stood at her door, she called out again and again. When she tried the doorknob, it was locked. Swearing to herself, she settled back into her bed again. Yet, for the first time, she wondered if they would really leave her here. And for how long would they abandon her?

She had no answers, but, if this was their way of disposing of a troublesome person they didn't really want to kill, maybe they wouldn't be back. If she was stuck here without food or water, how long could she last? Three days maybe? What was it for water, four?

What a terrible way to die. Not that there was ever a good way to die, but this was not how she wanted to go out. She wanted to do too many things in life. Just then she sensed something rummaging around outside. She hesitated, then walked to her door again and called out, "Hello? Hello?"

Again all she heard was silence. Then somebody tried the doorknob, but it was locked from their side too. Then came a voice, a voice she recognized, calling out, "Amy?"

"Wallace," she cried out. "Is that you?"

"Yeah, it's me. Hang on. And stand back." After a sharp series of kicks, the door came down.

She burst into tears when she saw him and threw herself into his arms. He wrapped her up tight and just held her close for a moment. "I don't know where they are," she muttered. "A little while ago I heard a noise, maybe a silent alarm or something. Then it seemed as if everybody just left. I called out several times, but nobody answered."

"Yeah, I wondered if somebody had caught sight of me," Wallace admitted, "but I couldn't stop looking for you."

"I can't believe you found me," she murmured, tightly wrapping her arms around him.

"I did, but I am not at all comfortable staying here," he shared, pulling her toward the doorway. "I don't know if they're coming back or if they have set a trap. However, I do know that, if they were alerted to my presence, … there's no reason for them *not* to come back after us."

"They're looking for you," she stated. "Although I don't know that they came right out and confirmed that."

"I know they are," he murmured, as he pulled her closer and out of the room she had been held in.

As soon as they stepped outside of this general area into another *hallway*, she gasped. "What is this place?"

"Sewer lines," he told her. "A whole city is down here, and your kidnappers have been using these rooms quite freely. So let's get you out of here quickly. Are you able to run?"

She stared around, taking in the toxic smell and nodded. "The faster, the better," she muttered. "God, this is gross, and we need to leave."

"Yeah, I don't know if your room was a control room, a meeting room, a staff room, or what. I have no idea," he noted, "but that little area was a whole lot cleaner than the rest."

"This explains the dampness, the chill," she shared.

He gave her a smile and reached out a hand. "I do know of a couple other tunnels to get us out of here fast. I just don't want to go out the way that they've been using."

"Just go," she urged. "I'll follow along."

He gave her a bright smile. "You've always been such a trooper." With that, he picked up the pace and started to run.

She ran at his side, sometimes barely managing to stay on her feet because the ground underneath was so slippery. Several times she thought she would fall, but Wallace managed to hang on to her and to keep her upright. When they finally came to a stop, she gasped. "Oh my God, this place seems to go on and on forever."

"It does," he confirmed. "It goes on for a long way, but …" Then he looked around. "I think a Y is up ahead, and they've been taking the one to the side, so I want to go in the opposite direction."

"I want to go wherever they're not," she declared in a harsh tone.

"Yep, you and me both. We just have to make it to the Y." He gave her a smile and squeezed her hand. "Come on." Almost immediately they came upon it. He pointed at the footsteps and shared, "They're all going out that way. It is a faster route. But …"

"No, no," she said, hating everything about that path. "Let's go the opposite way."

"That's the plan." He pulled her along in the opposite direction.

She asked, "How did you even find me?"

"It's a long story, but we found another man who pointed us in this direction, who had been held by the same group of kidnappers. At least that's what we believe."

She gasped. "Is he okay?"

"Yes and no. He's been badly injured, so we took him out of here, and Riff headed up top with him. We had to carry him because he had a lot of broken bones, but he should be at the hospital by now," Wallace added. "I figured after I talked to him that you were still out here because they were talking about grabbing you. He was unlucky enough to be mistaken for me and suffered terribly for absolutely nothing. I knew then that his kidnappers were most likely the ones who had taken you."

"All they could talk about was this new government

agency," she muttered.

"The new MI6 group?"

"Yes, and it's attracted quite a bit of interest, but it's BS because they want to start their own group."

"Do they know that you can do some of this stuff?" he asked, casting her a glance.

"I can't do anything, as you very well know," she muttered.

He gave her a gentle smile. "And they believed you?"

"I hope so. They locked me away again and didn't really give me any information as to what they would do with me," she muttered. "So maybe I was just fooling myself. I can't believe they just left me there."

"They left you there, probably assuming that you would get found," Wallace pointed out. "After all, I think I was spotted in their area. So I'm not convinced that their intent was to leave you to die."

She felt a little better. "One was called Dominic. He was supposedly a mind reader, according to what he told me anyway. He kept insisting that I was thinking about you. And why wouldn't I be when it was so obvious that they were targeting people who had been at the MI6 meeting? Dom didn't seem to like my having answers to give back to him, but I did tell him about what had happened to me, and I think they did believe me at that point in time," she admitted. "I also think they were a little bewildered and seemed to struggle as they tried to figure out what to do with me."

"Of course, so maybe my coming along when I did was good timing for them to leave."

"Maybe. It was certainly good timing for me," she admitted, with a happy sigh. "You have no idea how grateful I am to not be in there anymore. I'm glad I didn't realize how gross it was just outside my little area. That would have made my time there much worse."

He squeezed her hand gently. "Believe me, that ever since we found out you'd gone missing, we've been on the hunt. We got slowed down when we had no idea that you'd requested a new room at the hotel." He turned and glared at her. "You really should tell people these things, by the way."

"I would have if I'd had anybody to tell," she replied, "or, you know, if only I'd known I was about to be kidnapped." She snorted.

He nodded. "That's the thing, isn't it? We never really know when shit is about to happen."

"Exactly," she agreed. She kept hanging on to his hand as they made their way, quickly walking farther and farther down the tunnels. "You sure you have some idea where we are?"

"Can you see my footprints?" he asked.

"No, I can't see anything," she said in exasperation.

"Use your other eyes," he invited.

"Oh." She stopped in place for a moment, then shifted her perception and almost laughed. "My God, they're practically glowing."

"Pretty much," he confirmed. "It's a bit of a trick I learned a while back for finding my way around in the jungle. I managed to get my footprints to fluoresce, so I can follow them in and out again."

"That's amazing," she cried out.

He laughed. "I don't know about amazing, but it sure helps in these situations, although all we're really doing is walking in a straight line here." He shrugged. "We should come to the surface soon."

"You really did come a long way looking for me," she noted in amazement, turning around.

"Of course," he replied, squeezing her hand. "I'd hardly leave you to these guys."

"A lot of people would have, you know," she murmured.

"But not me, and you know that, right?"

She gave a happy sigh, squeezing his hand. "I really, really, really appreciate it." When he gave her a hard look, she sighed. "I know. You don't want gratitude, *blah-blah-blah*."

He laughed. "The things you remember."

"You made it pretty clear the last time I saw you."

"What?" he protested. "I did no such thing."

"You told me that you didn't want gratitude or to be seen as a hero. You didn't want anything like that. Even though you were my hero back then."

"BS," he replied, with a chuckle. "Let's face it. You were already way more adept at saving yourself than I ever would be."

"And yet so much in my world came crumbling down very, very quickly."

"Sometimes life is like that," he noted, his tone calm. "And often it's all about how quickly you can pick yourself back up again."

"Sometimes you don't pick yourself up at all," she murmured. "It's just … it's hard. It hurts, and you can't really move very much with all that pain, physical or otherwise."

"Maybe so," he agreed. "On the other hand, you've done phenomenally well. So don't be so hard on yourself."

"Sure, sure." She moaned. "Then I lost track of you and everybody else."

"That was by choice, wasn't it?"

"Sure. I was dealing with some tough stuff, and … I figured that everybody was better off without me."

Now he groaned at that. "Is that why you didn't get back to me?"

"Yeah," she said. "I didn't want to be a burden to anybody. When I lost my abilities—or thought I had way back when—that's what it felt like."

"But when you got them back again," he asked, turning to look at her curiously, "did you still think you didn't have any friends?"

"Pretty much, and then I got really sick, and everything got weird."

"When you say *weird*, what does that mean exactly?" he asked, curious.

Just then came a shout up ahead, and, using his flashlight, Wallace could make out Riff coming toward them.

Riff took one look at her and grinned. "Glad to see he found you," Riff greeted her, with a smile.

"Hi. Believe me that I'm very grateful he did."

"Yeah, that was pretty nasty," he noted, "and you can bet that MI6 wants to know all about it."

She groaned at that. "Of course they do."

"What they'll want to know is what happened, who did this to you, and what connection it has with MI6," Riff explained.

She shrugged. "I don't think my kidnappers have any connection to MI6, but I think they're using MI6 resources to find people who have abilities, so they can set up their own energy-working team."

"Which follows along with what we were wondering," Riff agreed, with a nod, looking over at Wallace.

"It does, but it sucks," Wallace noted, "because I don't know how many other people Jonas and his guys had that they were talking to, but if it was just us? ... Then the possibility exists that MI6 already had a leak in the sense that some other guy, some poor other guy named Wallace was picked up as me, and then Amy was picked up as well. She's convinced them, we hope, that she has lost her abilities, and they think they've got one up on MI6."

"I did tell my kidnappers that, if I had been a viable candidate, MI6 never would have let me leave until they had me all locked down and certainly wouldn't have just dropped me off at a hotel. The kidnappers seemed to believe that line more than anything."

Wallace frowned at her and nodded. "That is the truth too."

She frowned back at him. "Really? So, I already failed then?"

He laughed. "No. It's not that you failed. There was no failing. It seems to me that is one of those things that they're still trying to sort out the viability of."

"No, it's past that," she argued. "MI6 was already making inquiries with other people, meaning that it was well past the point of their still deciding if I was a worthwhile candidate. I think we were being actively interviewed, and I just didn't make the cut." She stopped and then laughed. "God, can you imagine, ... failing at that, something that's tormented me my entire life, and here even now is still causing me hell? I wasn't even going to talk to them about it, until I decided that I should probably reconnect with the world around me, especially after being so ill and having so many changes happening." She shook her head. "A bloody nuisance, the whole lot of it is." Up ahead she saw a bit of light. "Please tell me that's daylight out there."

"It is," Riff confirmed. "What we can't be sure of,

though, is that we're alone."

At that, she sucked in her breath, stared at him, and asked, "What do you mean?" Her voice was a harsh whisper.

"If the kidnappers know you guys were being interviewed, and they also know that Wallace here was about to disturb them, what are the chances that they have been following you or us—or me for that matter—and aren't waiting up ahead?" Riff suggested. "We can't take a chance of running into them."

"That's lovely," she muttered, as she stopped in her tracks and turned to stare at him. "What do you suggest we do then? This isn't exactly where I want to spend the rest of the day. I want to go home and have a shower." She sniffed the air around them and winced. "Definitely a shower."

"A shower would be lovely," Riff agreed. "We just have to confirm that we aren't followed from here."

"How do we do that, when I don't even know where these guys came from? And they took me from my hotel. I thought for the longest time that it was some test by MI6, thinking they would get to see me use my abilities to get out of this."

Riff stared at her for a moment. "That's an interesting idea," he noted. "One we've also been considering. I'm still not so sure these kidnappers have the brains to do something as advanced as that though."

She snorted. "I see you're a big fan too."

"Not so much," he said, with a wry smile. "I prefer private over government any day. Government does this shit all the time and never even apologizes," he noted, with a headshake. "And, no, I don't know that's what this was all about. However, as soon as we get back to civilization, we'll have to let MI6 know that we have you, and you will have to answer some questions."

"Do I really have to though?" she muttered, with a shake of her head. "I'm not sure I owe them a damn thing. I didn't really want to come over, but coming over is one thing, while getting kidnapped after somebody found out about their super top secret meeting is another," she added in a mocking tone. "If MI6 has leaks like that, they surely aren't safe enough to work for. I don't appreciate getting kidnapped as a result of their leaky ship."

"I agree," Riff replied, "and I'm certainly prepared to back you, should you want to argue it. Yet I think you'll find it a whole lot easier to just go through the exit interview process, regardless of how much information you choose to give them."

"It's not as if I can give them much anyway," she said.

"Did the kidnappers keep their faces hidden?"

"No, they didn't—or their voices either for that matter," she shared. Then she stopped and nodded. "That just supports the idea that they probably weren't planning to come back for me."

"It's possible," Wallace interjected, as he approached the entrance of the tunnel. "I wouldn't want to think of them doing that, but seeing their faces means either you wouldn't be allowed a chance to confirm who they were or they had no worries about your doing that."

While she pondered exactly what that meant, she heard a shout up ahead. As they stepped out into the sunlight, they were suddenly surrounded.

WALLACE, AMY, AND Riff were quickly placed in vehicles

and escorted back to MI6 HQ. As they walked into the building, escorted by a man on either side, Jonas impatiently waited for them. When Jonas laid eyes on Amy, Wallace watched the relief cross Jonas's face. "It's a damn good thing I saw the relief on your face," he snapped, "because we're still contemplating whether you're behind all this in the first place."

Jonas stared at him, his jaw dropping. "What?" he cried out. "You're still hanging on to that nonsense?"

"If you're testing people to see what they can do, … this would be one hell of a good way to do it," Amy stated. "So, yeah, it did cross my mind that you might have been behind this."

"Dear God," he muttered, "it's not as if any government operation will sanction something like that."

She laughed. "Are you sure about that? Seems to me you guys sanction all kinds of shit, and it's not as if you wait or look for approval before you do." He flushed at that and then glared at her. She waved her hand about. "Don't mind me. I'm just a little cranky after being kidnapped, held against my will, then running for my life through the sewers."

"Did they do anything to you?" he asked.

"No, they didn't," she muttered, "unless of course kidnapping qualifies. But I got the definite impression—when they all took off and left me alone—that they weren't coming back and that I was an easily disposable item."

Jonas nodded. "I wouldn't be at all surprised. When it comes to those for-hire groups, if you don't fit what they want, they don't want anything to do with you."

"Yeah, and what they wanted was to set up a team. Apparently just the same as you've been talking about," she muttered. "The question is, who the hell in your organization is giving away your secrets? Why would I even want anything to do with a company, a government, that can't even keep its own employees safe, particularly when we didn't even get through the interview process?" she asked, with a snort. "But now you're off the hook since I know you were letting me down easy by dropping me off at the hotel."

Jonas's jaw worked several times as he processed all the information she was sending his way, the pace of it making his head spin. He shook his head. "I didn't say you wouldn't be part of the team," he muttered. "I was trying to figure out where to go from here and was taking Wallace to the hotel."

"Maybe," she conceded, "but I definitely felt I didn't make the grade. Then, when I got kidnapped, I couldn't help but wonder if you guys hadn't set it up as some crazy testing scenario."

"We didn't," Jonas confirmed in a short and testy tone.

"You didn't?" she asked again. "Anybody else in your group who may have?"

He looked at her in surprise and then shook his head. "If you mean another government department, no," he replied. "That's just not how we operate."

She didn't say anything to that because, as far as she was concerned, it was exactly how they operated.

Wallace kept an arm around her as they headed up to the offices. He looked over at Jonas. "You've got one hour, and then she needs to go to the hotel to shower and to rest, if not take a swing by the hospital to get checked over."

She glared at him at that suggestion. "No," she snapped. "I need a shower, that's all. I could use it well before this, but I don't want to come back, so let's get this over with. Then get me out of here," she muttered. She turned to face Jonas, plastered on a smile, and added, "*Please.*"

He laughed. "I'll do my best."

"And considering that Wallace and Riff found me," she conceded, "obviously your best is pretty damn fine." And, on that note, she glared at Jonas. "What is it you want to know?"

"I need to know who it was and what they said to you."

"Almost nothing. One was called Dominic. I don't know any other names, but there were five of them in total—Dom, their psychic, then three minions serving as guards, plus the boss man." She gave her basic perceptions of them and added, "There was talk about mind reading and various other abilities. They seemed to think that I had some abilities, but I tried hard to convince them I didn't. I salted it with the truth about a car accident I had many years ago, which is when my abilities came into play, along with the fact that I also lost them a few years later," she muttered.

At that, Jonas stared at her, fascinated.

"Apparently you didn't know that either," she noted, with a headshake. "The kidnappers had done some research on me, and they were damn accurate but with some holes. It pissed me off, but they hadn't heard any of these earlier details."

"No, of course not," Jonas muttered. "I didn't know those details."

"You weren't looking in Brazil, which is where I was at the time of the car accident and where these abilities started to show up," she shared.

"When did they stop?"

"When I hit puberty," she replied, angrily glaring at him now. "How is it that you brought me in for a job interview, but you don't know all this?"

"Because we didn't do that deep of an investigation," he shared, "not yet anyway. We were trying to figure out if it was even something worth doing and who out there had the abilities to make this team possible," he explained. "It seems as if you *special* guys are also pretty closed-mouthed about it all."

"Yeah, and I wonder why," she declared, with a snort.

Wallace just laughed, walked over, sat her down on a chair, then stepped behind her, placing his hands on her shoulders. "That's fifteen minutes of your one hour," he announced to Jonas.

Jonas glared at him, but he shrugged. "Hey, fair is fair."

"Damn straight," Wallace stated. "She's exhausted and obviously has been through a hell of an ordeal already. I'm certain that she feels as if she stinks of the sewer that we dragged her out of, as do Riff and I," Wallace added, "and—until she gets a shower, a hot cup of coffee, some decent food, she won't even start to unwind. Right now she's tense, frustrated, and edgy. I just want to get her back to the hotel."

"Not that hotel," she declared, twisting to look up at him in horror.

"No, absolutely not that hotel," he agreed, with a smile. "I've even thought that maybe we should take you straight over to Terk's place." He turned to Riff, who was leaning against the door and studying the group.

Riff nodded. "Let me talk to him." And, with that, he stepped out of the room.

She frowned as she looked up at Wallace. "I'm not sure that's a good idea."

He shrugged. "You need a place to go to that is safe. You need a place to heal, and I know that you've already had some conversation with Terk about the shifts in your gifts."

They both turned to face Jonas. Wallace nudged him. "You're running out of time."

Jonas glared at Wallace. With a sigh, he turned to Amy. "This Dominic, would you recognize him again?"

"I would probably recognize all of them again," she replied, "but I didn't recognize them in terms of knowing who they are, if that's what you're asking."

"Right. Would you look at some books for us?"

She nodded, and he quickly walked over to a computer, punched some keys, and a screen appeared on the wall. Then he opened a series of mug shots but more official-looking. "Let me know as these photos run by if you see anyone who looks familiar."

She nodded, and even Wallace watched as the faces shifted rapidly around them. She called out, "Wait."

"That one?" Jonas hit Stop.

"No, go back one."

He went back one, and she nodded. "So that could be Burly."

"Burly?" he repeated in confusion.

"Yeah, the angry burly guy seemed to be the leader of the men. I don't mean that's his name. That's just how I thought of him."

"This guy is wanted by Interpol," Jonas noted. "So that would make sense. Although I don't know what he's doing, getting involved with this. He's KGB though, *ex*-KGB, and the last we have on him is that he's now gone private."

"He was there, and Dominic was there, but I haven't seen a picture of him yet," she murmured. "Maybe you don't have one. Then two of the three guards almost looked as if they could be related. Brothers maybe or cousins, I don't know. But they were definitely down the pecking order. I think Burly was the boss of the henchmen. I think Dominic—who seemed arrogant all the time, as if he had an ability himself, or wanted people to think so—he reported to Burly too. Dom mentioned how he could read minds, and the others seemed a little afraid of him. Maybe not afraid, but a little leery because they didn't really know what he could do. I think he was using the mind reader moniker to keep the others from getting too close to him—in case he really could read their minds."

"Smart," Wallace conceded, with a nod. "The last thing anybody wants is to have somebody around who can read what's on their mind."

"So, I'm not sure that he was a mind reader or just a good fake," she murmured, "but, … from a few things he said, it's possible he has a gift."

"Right," Wallace muttered, "that makes sense." He turned to Jonas. "Why would this Burly guy be involved in this?"

"He's private, so he was probably just hired to find and to put together a team. However, his problem will be the same as ours, finding anybody with abilities."

"He did say that," she shared, with a smile, "and I just assumed that they were trying to piggyback off your research."

He nodded. "Sounds like it."

She stood up, her legs shaky. Wallace reached out with a supporting arm. She smiled at him and muttered, "I really need to go lie down now." She turned back to Jonas. "If you have more questions, just let Wallace know, and he can get ahold of me, but I'm done for now." And, with that, she turned and headed for the door.

Jonas raced behind her. "Wait."

She turned to glare at him. "What?"

"We really didn't have anything to do with this," he repeated, "and we're very sorry it happened."

She nodded. "*Sorry* doesn't really cut it right now though. I just want to go someplace where I'm safe and don't smell the sewer and don't have to face these *lovely* aspects of life," she muttered. "There's a reason I walked away from this thing years ago." Leaving Jonas standing there, staring at her, with more questions on his lips, she walked out, finding Riff there to join her.

Jonas turned to Wallace, who was only a couple steps behind. "What happened to her?"

He hesitated, then replied, "You really do need to do more research on her, but she used to help the cops a lot. It was always very ugly cases, like missing kids, rapes, murders, things like that. She eventually just burned out," he added. "Anybody who does that for any amount of time, regardless of their abilities or talents, they burn out, and they carry it all with them and suffer terribly from PTSD." Wallace shrugged. "That's why she's blocked off a ton of it for a long time now."

"But then when she got sick, I thought things changed. I thought something happened then."

"Yeah, it certainly did. Her abilities came back full force. Stronger, better. Or maybe *badder* is a better word," he clarified, with a laugh. "She's still trying to figure it all out."

"So, she's good? I know I asked you before," Jonas muttered, with a wave of his hand. "I guess I'm asking again. Is she good?"

"Yes, she's good," Wallace confirmed, "as in seriously good. Now, if you'll excuse me, I'm taking her someplace safe."

At that, he walked out of the room, leaving Jonas staring behind them.

CHAPTER 5

W HEN THEY PULLED up in front of the castle doors in the huge roundabout driveway, Amy was shocked. She leaned forward and muttered, "Seriously?"

Riff laughed. "Yes, seriously."

It was late and dark, but the castle had lights all around that gave it an eerie, almost haunted glow. As they got out, she looked back at Wallace. "Are you sure about this?"

He nodded.

Just then the castle's front door opened, and a tall figure was outlined there. Riff sighed. "Hello, Angela."

She glared at him. "Well?"

He shook his head. "No, not yet."

She turned and walked back inside.

At that, Amy looked back at Wallace. "That's not an auspicious beginning."

He shrugged. "It is what it is. Don't make it more than that."

She wasn't sure what that meant, but she could do only so much about it anyway. So she walked inside to find a lot of people sitting around a massive table, all talking. The conversations died when they entered, but one man, whom she recognized—more on instincts than anything else—got up and walked over, separating himself from the crowd. He opened his arms, and, when she fell into them, they closed around her securely, almost with a sense of homecoming.

She tilted her head back and whispered, "Hi, Terk."

He smiled, leaned down, and whispered, "Hi back." He held her shoulders and smiled at her. "Come on. Let's get you upstairs."

"What about everybody here?" she asked, looking behind him.

"No need to worry about that now," he said, "Tomorrow will be soon enough. An awful lot of people live here, and you don't need to deal with that just now. Take your time and get some rest."

She nodded and whispered, "Thank you."

He just smiled and escorted them upstairs via an elevator. That setup was way more modern than the castle appeared to be from the outside. By the time they got to a room, he pushed open the door and announced, "This is a suite, with two rooms, that you and Wallace can share. As you can see, it's got an adjoining living area and an en suite bathroom. So, Wallace, once you have a chance to settle in, come on down, and we'll send some food up for you two."

She was so grateful for his consideration.

Terk looked down at her and added, "I don't expect to see you until morning, do you hear?"

She smiled and whispered, "Are you sure?"

"I'm sure. You've had more than enough to deal with. We're not putting more on your plate tonight." With that, he said good night and quickly disappeared.

She stared behind him and told Wallace, "I forgot how nice he always is."

"I would imagine so. Remember that he can read your energy and a hell of a lot more. He probably can tell how exhausted you are, how emotionally worn out, and lots of other things that you and I can't even imagine yet. He knows what you've been through, so he's being a kind, compassionate, empathetic person."

"I get that," she admitted, "but I was still expecting to have to socialize. While I'm not feeling quite up to it, it was nice that he didn't put me through it."

"It was." Wallace dropped their bags in their respective bedrooms.

"I'm so exhausted. I don't know if I should just … collapse or have a shower."

They walked into the bathroom together, and she gasped. "My God," she muttered. "It's huge."

"It is nice." He looked around, then pointed out the tub. "Unless you want a bath instead of a shower."

She stared at it in delight, a great big stone claw-foot bathtub, but fully modernized. "I absolutely love it," she exclaimed and nodded. "I think a bath would be a great idea. I could completely destress in all that water." As she eyed the assortment of bubble baths on the side, she nodded. "I'm definitely heading for a bath."

He leaned over, turned on the water, checked the temperature, and nodded. "Go ahead and add what you want. I'll clean up a little, then head downstairs and see about some food."

"I don't even think I could eat," she added, turning to him. "Especially not if it means going downstairs."

"I don't think you have to go downstairs," he said, "but I'll go check it out." She smiled at that, and he closed the door behind him, as he headed off to his part of the suite.

She slid into the hot water, almost groaning in relief. Her body had been chilled deep inside from her time in the tunnels, a chill that she hadn't fully noted until now, when she had been able to do something about it. Her body had shut down, not able to cope in that terrible place. Now here, everything was so big and so overwhelmingly beautiful. She just collapsed into the water, closed her eyes, and rested.

It must have been at least thirty minutes later when she heard a knock on the door. "Who is it?"

Wallace answered with a laugh, "It's me. I hope you're not expecting anybody else."

"Come in."

He hesitated at the doorway. "Are you covered?"

"I am, at least I think so."

He came in a little bit closer, setting a small coffee table beside her. "I brought you a cup of coffee. I know it's late, but it was either that or herbal tea."

"Coffee is fine," she murmured. "It never affects me."

"Good for you. They're sending us up a couple plates in a bit, just something light," he added, "so I'll be back in a few minutes."

"Do I have to get out?" she asked, twisting to look up at him.

"Nope, I don't see why you would need to," he said, "especially if you don't want to. So you might as well eat in the tub if you're comfortable." He shrugged.

"Sounds good to me."

And, with that, he was gone.

She laughed, as it sounded good to her too. Damn good. Too good to be true. She didn't think she'd ever had a meal in a bathtub before. But right now, still loath to move, anything that allowed her to stay up to her chin in a bubble bath was just fine.

When Wallace returned a little bit later, he had a small plate on a small tray in his hands. She'd finished the coffee, and he quickly removed that and put down the tray. "Here's a bowl of soup and a meat pie," he said. "Do you want it here, or are you ready to come out?"

She contemplated it and nodded. "I think I need to get out. As much as I don't want to, I've had enough."

"Then I'll take this out in the other room and wait for you," he murmured and quickly disappeared around the corner.

After scrubbing down from head to toe, including her hair, she got up, dried off, wrapped her hair in a towel, snatched up the robe and pajamas that had been provided for her, and dried off a little bit before getting dressed. She then headed into the other room. Wallace was sitting down at a small table for two, with the plates of food.

She smiled. "I don't know what I expected, but I wasn't expecting hotel treatment."

"I think it's just a matter of whatever is available to eat under these circumstances," he said, with a smile. "And, in this case, they just happened to have soup to warm up and some meat pies left over."

"Sounds good." She sat down, tasted the soup, then groaned. "Wow, I hadn't realized I was so hungry."

"Eat," he urged.

She quickly dove into the food. When she lifted her head a few minutes later, she realized half the soup was gone already. She looked over at him, shamefaced. "Sorry. ... I didn't even say *thank you*."

"I think you did." He chuckled. "It really doesn't matter anyway. Keep eating and enjoy it."

"I will," she murmured, as she quickly dropped her head and finished the soup. Then she sat back and rubbed her tummy. "The flavor's absolutely to die for. But then again, as hungry as I was, it could have been terrible, and I wouldn't have noticed. Yet it was delicious." She picked up a fork and had a bite of her meat pie as she looked over at his. "Did you get enough? They only gave you a little soup and one meat pie too?"

Wallace nodded. "I'm good."

She asked, "What about Riff?"

"I think Riff has a room here. The woman who met him at the door? They've got some relationship history, but I don't know the details. I'm not sure what the deal is because nobody talks about it, and nothing was mentioned about them tonight."

"Right, everybody here has their own personal lives. That's the thing to remember, isn't it?"

"Everybody everywhere has a personal life," he clarified, with a smile. "We just aren't always privy to what that means to the individuals."

"Right. Just like you?"

"I don't have a life anywhere, remember?" he shared, with a laugh.

"You always had short-term relationships. You never wanted anything longer than that. Has that changed?"

"Nope, still don't." He shrugged. "I'm happy as I am."

"Are you though?"

He smiled at her. "I have been, up until now at least."

She laughed. "If that's a hint ..."

"Not necessarily a hint, just saying that I'm not against opening myself up to a relationship in the future," he explained, still smiling. "I'm not in any rush, and we'll see where things go. Right now, I just want to stay safe."

"Right, because that asshole will be coming after you too, won't he?"

"I'm hoping they're completely discouraged from coming after any of us," he declared, shooting her a look. "The last thing we need is to watch our backs constantly."

"I agree," she replied, "and I would like to think that they'll ignore us now that they've lost me. However, they went to a lot of effort to get you, then got the wrong guy. So, I imagine they won't give up that easily, not now that they know they're on the right track to the real Wallace guy they wanted."

He nodded slowly. "It is a consideration," he murmured. "That's another reason for both of us to keep up our strength, just in case they try again."

"They better not," she murmured, "because, this time, I'll be ready."

WHEN WALLACE WOKE up the next morning with a sudden start, it took a minute to realize where he was and how he'd gotten here. Right on the heels of that thought was a worry as to how Amy's night had been. He got up, walked through the living room to the other bedroom door, and opened it quietly.

He was hoping she was still sound asleep. As he peered in and didn't see her on the bed, he scanned the room and saw her curled up on the couch, instead of in bed, which is where he'd last seen her. He walked over to check on her.

She opened her eyes and looked up at him. She shrugged. "I'm fine, but I woke up way too early and then couldn't get back to sleep."

"Have to love all those thoughts in your head, right?" he murmured.

"No, I really don't," she stated, followed by a yawn. "You look better rested."

He nodded. "I slept pretty well, though I'm quite surprised that I didn't hear you get up."

"Doesn't matter," she muttered. "It's all quiet here, and nobody wanted us, needed us, or attacked us. So maybe it's a good thing that you got some sleep. You'll be more alert than I will."

"Did you get any sleep at all?"

"Sure," she noted, with a wry smile, "until 5:00 a.m. Then I was wide awake and knew I wouldn't go back to sleep again, so I just got up."

He nodded, walked over to the couch, and sat down beside her. "Do you need food?"

"I'm feeling very much like an unwelcome guest," she murmured. "Maybe not *unwelcome*, but it's an odd feeling being here, since I didn't really talk to anybody last night. I just allowed you and Terk to bundle me up and to take me away, so I could recover a little bit. ... And believe me that I'm very grateful, but now it feels very much as if I need to go down and meet everyone."

"Agreed. Give me a few minutes to shower, then I'll go down with you," he offered, realizing she probably would have just walked down without even thinking about it. If they were a little more comfortable here, it probably would have been totally fine.

He imagined that everybody treated this as their home, where you could walk around wearing whatever you wanted. However, when you're in somebody else's place, and not feeling terribly comfortable, that was a whole different story. He showered and dressed quickly. By the time he walked back out, she stood in the living room, waiting for him.

"I don't have any clothes," she reminded him.

"You do, just not very many."

"Sure," she conceded. "I have my travel bag. Thanks to Riff for picking it up. Still, my clothes are more suited for the office and interviews."

"Right." He nodded in understanding. "Not exactly jeans, *huh?*"

"No," she murmured, "but thankfully, here they stock the closets and bathrooms with essentials. Thus, this very fashionable jogging suit you see me in this morning."

He wrapped an arm around her shoulders, gave her a gentle hug, and stated, "I suspect they get a lot of unexpected visitors, who may come in with only the clothes on their backs. I will say that you look much better this morning than compared to last night."

She burst out laughing, as they stepped out of the room. "I would take that as a compliment, except I was such a freaking mess when I arrived here that it would have been really challenging to have looked worse."

He was still grinning as they headed downstairs. She hesitated at the base of the stairs, and he nudged her toward the noise. "In this place, you can always follow the sound of people gathering to a kitchen."

"How do you know it's the kitchen?"

"Because that's where the heart of every home is," he said, with a smile. "And, in this case, an awful lot of people live here, so the kitchen, dining room, or whatever you want to call it, will be where everybody is."

Sure enough, as they came around the corner, at least a dozen people sat at the huge dining table. Immediately silence filled the room.

She winced and stood in front so everybody could see

her, then nodded in a formal way and greeted everyone. "Good morning. I'm Amy, and I want to thank you all for the hospitality."

Several women hopped up and walked over to her, smiling. "You're more than welcome," said one of them. "We would introduce ourselves, but you'll forget all our names in five minutes."

Amy burst out laughing. "I doubt I would even make it that long."

Wallace spied the coffee service over on the side, and he headed over toward it.

One of the women laughed. "Clearly you know what's important in the morning."

"At this hour of the day? Definitely," he agreed, with a smile, that turned into a yawn.

Terk spoke from behind him. "Did you guys get any sleep?"

Wallace nodded, then turned to him and smiled. "I did pretty well. Amy didn't though. She woke up early."

"To be expected," Terk noted, studying her carefully.

She didn't appear to have any problems staring right back at him though.

Wallace watched the interchange with amusement. Amy was unique, and an awful lot was going on in her system that not everybody understood. Yet she'd always been amiable and easy to get along with, and he knew she would fit in very quickly here. As he brought over two cups of coffee and placed one in front of her, she looked at it and smiled.

"Thank you," she murmured, sending him a grateful look. "You don't realize just how much coffee matters until you do without it."

"Some of us are coffeeholics," Riff interjected, walking

through the adjoining kitchen door, carrying a big cup and a plate laden with something that smelled suspiciously like cinnamon buns.

Everybody else seemed to feel the same way, and, as the aroma hit the table, several people bolted to their feet and raced into the kitchen.

Wallace sat down beside him. "I presume those are hard to come by."

"Hard to come by and even harder to keep," he shared, chuckling. "Don't worry. I knew what I was starting when I came out with this one."

Amy sat beside Riff. "Of course you did. Anything to cause trouble," she teased.

"Hey, I'm not into causing trouble," he replied, with a wry chuckle. "Besides, you should be nice to me. I helped get you out of there, remember?"

"You did, indeed," she agreed, with a smile. "And, for that, you can have my cinnamon bun."

He looked at her and brightened. "You would have to go get it though," he noted. "I already took two, so that's all I'm allowed. However, if you got yours, then gave it to me …"

She rolled her eyes at the hungry expression on his face and asked, "Do you really need three?"

"Of course I need three," he declared, rubbing his tummy. "We all do, and anybody who could pull that off? They would absolutely do it in a heartbeat." He chuckled, nudging her gently.

Just then Terk came out with a large plateful of them. She stared at the tower of buns on his plate and gaped. He glared at her. "No, my excuse is valid, and no one can deny it. I use it for energy."

"*Uh-huh,*" she muttered, frowning, looking around the

table at the others who all seemed to be working on their own large plates of sugar. "Did you at least start with steak and eggs or something before you go into this level of sugar?"

"No, that'll come afterward," he said. "I've already done a ton of work this morning."

He didn't look tired, and, the more she saw of him, she realized that he did look more energized. "It was energy work, from the looks of you."

"Exactly, hence, I'm burning low."

"So, that's your story, and you're sticking to it?"

He burst out laughing and nodded. "Absolutely, so don't try to take my cinnamon buns away from me," he stated in alarm.

"Oh, no, I wouldn't dare. I already got the message loud and clear that apparently cinnamon buns are a major commodity around here."

At that, Wallace leaned over and asked, "Do you want one?"

She grimaced. "I wouldn't dare. I didn't do anything to deserve it, and these guys are all plowing through them at a pretty high rate." She just shook her head. "I sure hope you have a full-time cook."

"We just hired a full-time chef," Terk confirmed, with a nod. "Up until then, Mariana's been doing a ton of it, with just a couple assistants. So I know she's more than ready to hand some of it off as well."

"Yeah, I would think so," Amy muttered. "Feeding all you guys would have to be a full-time job."

"It is," declared a smiling woman, coming in with a small cinnamon bun and a cup of coffee. "I'm Mariana. I can confirm that it's a very full-time job." She looked over at Terk and suggested, "I think we need to make some changes to some of the apartments."

"What changes?" Terk asked warily.

"I think we need more playrooms for the kids," she suggested. "A little more of a homeschool setup and potentially … what about that outdoor playground?"

He nodded. "An awful lot of outdoor stuff still needs to be done, but we're hitting that budget line pretty hard."

She laughed. "You say that every time, no matter what I ask for or what I say we need." She chuckled. "You've got that part down pat."

"I might have it down pat, but it sure doesn't seem as if anybody listens."

She nudged his plate closer. "Funny, you don't complain about the food budget."

"He does," countered another woman, coming in with a smile. She had a small dainty cup in her hand as she sat down beside Terk. She looked over at their newest occupant and nodded. "Good morning, Amy. It's a pleasure to meet you."

Amy flushed. "Thank you for having me. It's been a difficult few days."

"Yeah, that crap has a way of hurting, doesn't it?"

And such a wealth of empathy filled her tone that Amy knew without a doubt that this woman had also been through something horrifically traumatic. "I think the thing that bothers me the most is the fact that these people seem to think they have every right to do whatever they want to people, and it doesn't matter whether you agree or not."

"Hear, hear," she muttered.

Mariana smiled and added, "I won't argue that one. It seems that we've all been through something horrific and traumatizing, so you're in good company here. We all empathize with what you've been through. We know what it feels like, to some degree at least, and, most important, we've all come out on the other side, much stronger and more resilient."

"I think Terk mentioned something about some of you having been ill or injured, and came out different?" Amy asked.

At that, Wallace wondered if he should turn the conversation to something else because of the instant silence in the room.

Amy winced. "Apparently that's not a question I should have asked." Wallace squeezed her hand gently. She looked over at Wallace and smiled. "Always looking after me, aren't you?"

"Hey, you know what they say about *save a life* ... and all."

She winced at that, picked up her coffee, and nodded. "Not exactly the way I wanted life to happen though."

"None of us would, but you have a life, so you get to make whatever changes you choose."

She chuckled at that. "That sounds great, if it didn't sound very much as if I wouldn't have a whole lot of choice."

"Choice is what you make of it," Terk declared, with that same cheerful voice he'd been using all morning. Terk then frowned over at Wallace.

Wallace shrugged. "Earlier Amy and I were discussing the fact that we don't think we're out of danger."

Terk stared at him for a moment and then slowly nodded. "I would have to agree."

Amy sucked in a breath and turned to him, Wallace still squeezing her fingers.

Wallace tilted his head. "Terk's just confirming what we already know."

She winced and nodded. "I know that, and in theory that should be great. In theory, but in reality, I would much rather have somebody say, *Hell no, you're perfectly safe,* or something of that nature."

"But that wouldn't be the truth, so you really wouldn't want that, right?" The comment came from one of the other women across the table.

Wallace thought it was Clary. She looked tired, as if she'd had a rough night. He frowned at her. "Looks as if you didn't get much sleep either."

She smiled. "Between the work we do and the babies we have, the family life," she noted, "a good night's sleep is hard to come by around here." She looked over at Amy. "Any experience with kids?"

Amy shook her head. "No, not so much, but I like them just fine."

"Hey, we'll take it," she muttered.

Wallace started to chuckle as Amy stared at her in surprise. "Sorry?" she asked cautiously.

Clary just waved a hand. "You'll get used to us. However, if you're around and if you have a few minutes to give one of the new mothers—or any of the mothers—a moment's rest, babysitters are always welcome."

Amy stared cautiously at the others. "How many children?"

At that Clary gave a laugh, but it was almost hysterical in nature. "Oh, I think thirteen so far," she shared, smiling. "They're all very young. Yet we also have Calum Jr., who is being an absolute sweetheart of a big brother to everybody." She laughed. "He might be a little confused when it comes to keeping all their names straight and who belongs to whom, but he really does care for all of them."

At that Mariana smiled and nodded. "I don't think he knows the names or relations either, but some days he wonders if it'll ever stop. Larry is also a great babysitter."

"Larry?" Wallace repeated.

Terk smiled. "Legend's half brother. You'll meet those two soon, if you haven't already."

Wallace just nodded.

"We needed more help with all the babies coming at basically the same time and seemingly all births are twins. So that should stop soon now," Terk explained. "We just had to get the proper mechanisms in place, like Angela."

"It took a while, as does everything it seems," said one of the guys from the far side of the room. "I'm Damon," he added, for Amy's benefit.

Wallace had heard rumors about Angela and Riff and knew a bit about what was going on with them. Wallace turned to Riff. "So, are you next?"

At that, silence fell again at the table.

CHAPTER 6

WALLACE WINCED. AMY might have made a gaffe herself, but what he had just mentioned appeared to put everybody in an uncomfortable position. Amy squeezed his fingers and gave him a bolstering smile. He shrugged. "Obviously this time I said something completely wrong."

Terk chuckled. "We can't really be worried about who'll say things around here, especially when it's the truth," he shared. "That is something we're all working our way into, finding a methodology that works here with all of us," he said, with a smile. "But I think we should turn our attention to what your plan is at this point."

"I don't have a plan," Amy stated boldly. "I was hoping somebody here would have an idea of how to get these guys off my back, or get this whole concept of a team off my back. Not to mention that another man was already tortured by mistake in Wallace's name," she told everyone. "So, it's not just me who's in danger. It's also Wallace."

"I heard about the other Wallace. He couldn't give you any other information?" Terk asked.

"He's in the hospital," Riff offered, "and was headed for surgery last night. I will get back in and talk to him today, but I'm not sure I'll be allowed in, at least not until he's a little bit better recovered."

"MI6 will be allowed in, so, if that's the case, you should

be allowed in," Terk declared, his tone hard, turning to face Wallace. "That poor man went through hell. For whatever reason they thought he was you."

"I was trying to figure that out because I don't know quite how it worked either. Jonas and I went to the hotel, dropping Amy off, which is why we didn't suspect Jonas, because he was with me."

"Nobody would suspect that," one of the men joked.

That brought a certain amount of laughter, but it was also a valid question in the sense that nobody quite understood how this other Wallace had been picked up. "We dropped off Amy, and then Jonas and I went to a pub and had a beer," Wallace shared. "It's possible that the other Wallace guy was there too. He did mention he'd been at a pub and had shared something about being in town for a job interview, then confirmed his name was Wallace. It's his last name though."

"It's quite possible he was there," Terk agreed, studying Wallace. "You'll need to track that down so you understand how this worked. Specifically how are they finding their victims?"

Wallace snorted. "Jonas was supposed to be looking into a mole or a leak in his department. ... I don't know how much effort will go into that."

Surprisingly Riff piped up. "I think he will be doing all he can. He was pretty upset that not only was Amy put through her ordeal but because this other completely innocent man suffered so badly as well. Jonas is angry about the whole thing. The mole might have a partner working in that hotel as well. So there is that possibility too." Riff looked over at Terk. "I wouldn't be at all surprised if you don't get a call from Jonas."

Terk nodded, staring at his phone. "Yeah, he'll call in a few minutes." He sighed. "Not sure we have a whole lot to tell him though."

"I don't think we have anything to tell him, but that won't stop him from calling and asking you to get more."

Amy's gaze went from one to the other. "Do you always work with MI6?"

"MI6, MI5, CIA, FBI, and other government agencies from all around the world," Terk stated. "We work with them all. Sometimes the work is easier than others." Terk sighed. "It all depends on the governments involved."

She couldn't imagine. "I had enough trouble, even coming to this interview," she murmured.

"Yet you came, so do you want to explain that?" Riff asked. "Because I don't understand. For somebody who was a child psychic but lost her abilities at puberty, then you suddenly show up for this job interview? How did Jonas find out about you, and why would you have considered going for the interview, even getting back into this work?"

She winced. "All very valid questions," she murmured, then groaned. "The first thing you must understand is that my abilities didn't really completely stop at puberty. It was my way of getting out of the circus that my family put me into."

At that, one of the women clapped. "Bravo, that was brilliant," she declared, "because everybody knows that at puberty everything is completely chaotic, so absolutely no guarantee of anything at that point in time. That was a perfect time to call it, and kudos to you for being so astute at that age."

Amy shrugged. "That's what I thought, so I didn't let anybody know that I still had the abilities, mostly out of guilt."

"Guilt?" asked the same woman. She then smiled and added, "I'm Celia, by the way. Terk is my husband."

Amy smiled at her. "Yeah, *guilt*," she confirmed, as she shrugged and shook her head. "While I was doing the work I was doing, at least I was helping all those people," she shared, "but it was costing me so much that I had to get out. I *had* to stop. I had to find a way to not be so completely wrecked by it all. Yet, once I was out of it, all I could think about was that I *should* be helping, that I could be doing more, so guilt and all set in. I just didn't know how to help them *and* to protect myself."

Celia smiled. "Conscience and heart," she noted, "a true sign of good people."

"Good people don't necessarily have good lives," Amy pointed out, "and that's part of the problem. I was desperate to have a life, and I still am. I'd been on that show-pony track for a long time, and I needed off. Plus, I did have an illness not all that long ago, and the consequences of that were even more shocking. I was contemplating doing something again with my abilities, wondering if it was all part and parcel of the same thing. Then I got quite ill, and my abilities became … *different*. But they were there." She grimaced. "It seemed serendipitous at the time that I heard about this job and was contacted."

Terk asked. "Did you fill out an application?"

She nodded. "I did."

"What did you put down for job experience?" Celia asked, with a note of laughter. "I can just imagine what Jonas was thinking."

"For a start, these were invitation only," Amy explained. "So that was a bit awkward. Obviously, once they realized who I was, they were interested in hearing if I had anything to say. Jonas did bring up the fact that I had supposedly lost all my abilities as a teenager."

"What did you tell him?" Terk asked.

"I told him the recent illness brought them back somewhat," she shared, with a shrug. "I wasn't sure what to say at that point and wasn't even sure I wanted him to pass on the news at all. I wasn't sure about any of it, honestly."

"Of course not."

"I was hoping to see Wallace," she admitted, looking over at him. "We had been friends before, and, as you can tell, we still are good friends—even though we hadn't been in contact for many a year. That's not a part of this at all, but it's frustrating to realize that somebody found out about me. It feels as if I'm very much back in that same show-pony thing again, only worse. I wouldn't be doing the bidding of people who might consider my welfare. Instead it would be people concerned only with their bottom line. Yet I'm driven to find a way to help people again." She shrugged. "I guess I'm looking for balance."

"You definitely felt that the kidnappers' plan was to force you to use your skills, right?" Terk asked.

She nodded. "They were talking about it—the one guy, whatever his name was." She frowned as she tried to remember that joker. "I can't even remember his name at the moment," she murmured.

"Dominic?" Wallace suggested.

"Ah." She nodded. "That's right. He was trying to test me in some way and was arrogant about his particular gifts. I didn't really understand what his game was, only that there was a game and that, as far as he was concerned, he was clearly the gamemaster. The four others around him felt as if nobody else knew anything about energy worker skills but

Dom, and they were definitely wary of him. It's always disconcerting when you have the wrong kind of people in the energy cycle." She looked over at Terk. "I'm sure you've seen it before."

He nodded. "I have, and usually they're the people you don't want to have around. Not to mention that too much ego just doesn't allow us to utilize their energy when we need to."

"How would you utilize Dom's energy?" she asked curiously.

"Sometimes, when we're on big jobs, we need to tap into other people's energy because we're flagging," Terk explained. "If you aren't okay with that, then you can't be part of a team."

"That's what a team would imply though," Amy noted. "That, as a team, when you're flailing, somebody else is there to step in, right? I could have used somebody on my team a long time ago," she murmured. "But what I had were nonbelievers and, … well, people who just didn't care. It wasn't about me. It wasn't about the victims or whoever I was trying to help at the time. It was only about them," she muttered, with a headshake. "I ended up with a really negative view of the world afterward."

"I can understand that."

"It took a while for them to realize and to accept that puberty had killed my abilities," she shared, with a twinkle in her gaze. "Maybe it wasn't fair to the rest of the world," she conceded, hating herself for being happy about it. "As you can tell, I'm still very conflicted about it."

"If you needed a break, you needed a break," Celia declared. "Whoever wasn't looking after you while you were doing all that work for everybody else was just a complete asshole."

"Make that plural," Amy clarified, "and that would be my parents." At that, everybody stared at her, and she shrugged. "There are many ways to parent, I guess. There are the helicopter parents, or then you have the ones who don't have a life, so they try to live through their kids. That was my parents. They didn't have a life. I appeared to have some ability, and, although they were extremely against it at the beginning, once the money started rolling in, they were the ones who wouldn't let me stop." Amy shook her head. "Their success, their self-identity, was tied to my success in closing cases. My success became their achievement, and they became addicted to it."

Amy continued. "You do get a very tainted view of life when you beg and plead to not have to face another grieving family and to find yet another dead child, then not be allowed to talk to anybody or to get any therapy because they didn't dare risk anybody finding out what my parents' part in all of it was. It was a very difficult time for me," Amy stated. "The only thing I could do, again with that feeling of guilt, was to just shut down." She was getting emotional, and her cheeks were flushed. "It seemed to be the only way I could make it work. Then, as I relaxed, I reopened to my gifts."

Terk clarified, "What you mean is, you shut down so you could heal." At that, everybody else nodded. "You did what you had to do for survival," Terk noted. "Never apologize for wanting to survive, and, although you were a child and had no say in the matter, you did what everybody asked of you, until you just couldn't do it anymore. That is not something you should feel guilty about."

Just hearing his input did so much for Amy's own peace of mind that she felt a tremendous weight sliding off her back.

Wallace turned to her and smiled. "Told you."

She glared at him. "Nobody likes a know-it-all."

He chuckled. "You do." She flushed and glared at him, but he just smiled. "I'll get you more coffee." With that, he hopped up and walked over to the coffee station and poured her another cup.

Everybody else sitting here now stared at her, and she flushed again. "Okay, now it feels as if you guys have questions, and I don't have a clue what you're looking for."

"Clarifying the relationship between the two of you would be nice," Celia suggested. "Obviously you are good friends, and I get the vibe. So is there anything more than that?"

"Yes and no," she replied. "We haven't had a proper chance to reconnect or to even figure out who we are anymore. So maybe ask me that question in another month or two."

"I will hold you to that," Celia stated. "Then the other burning question we all have is, what exactly did you do to help? You mentioned missing people, but was it just missing people or was it missing objects too? And how did that change as you grew after this recent illness?"

"Ah," Amy muttered. "Yes, it always comes down to those kinds of questions, doesn't it?" She couldn't help but turn bitter. "Sorry, it's a bit of a touchy subject for me, even now. It's tough to explain because they don't always have simple answers. I would like to tell you that I had all these definitive skills and that I could find missing people saying, *abracadabra,* and they would appear, but I can't." She shrugged. "Usually I closed my eyes and saw what was happening around that person, seeing a location where they currently lay, sat, were being held, whatever. Sometimes that worked. Sometimes it didn't. Sometimes I would be given an object of theirs and would see them in person and would be able to … I know it sounds stupid, but it's almost as if I could talk to them."

"It doesn't sound stupid at all," Wallace stated, "especially not in the present company."

"That's good," she muttered, "but, to be honest, it didn't always work. I guess it was me, but it seemed to depend on the other person too. Sometimes I could reach out and could tell them that help was on the way, to stay calm, that we were doing our best. Sometimes that made it better, and other times it made it worse."

"It was after one of those *worse* times that you decided you'd had enough, wasn't it?" Celia asked.

Amy turned to Celia and nodded slowly. "I'm not sure how you figured that out, but yes." She looked over at Wallace. "Maybe you can pick up that tale."

He nodded. "I knew about it from before. It's still painful obviously, but Amy went looking for a series of young girls who had gone missing," he began. "What she didn't realize was that, as she went looking, she didn't know anything about protecting herself, about keeping her energy close to her body, or that predators were out there with energy skills too. So, you can imagine what happened when this child molester, this murderer, realized somebody like Amy was coming after him. He managed to get a hold of her mentally, and it wasn't pretty at all. She managed to get free, but she was scarred for a very long time."

"And that's when I got strong enough to tell the rest of

my family and everybody else in the world to eff-off," she added. "Some traumas are just too difficult."

"Have you worked with the police at all since?" Celia asked.

"Anonymously," she replied, with half a smile. "But have I entered that arena again? Hell no. I've been holding back on it. Occasionally I do wonder about it because it was something I was good at."

"Was?"

"Am," she clarified, acknowledging it a bit tersely. "It's just not necessarily something I can do again, not in the same way as I did before."

"If you didn't have a ground and if you didn't have anybody there to help support you, with no loving support at home," Celia noted, her tone very soft, "then I can only imagine how it was for that child inside you, who was already asked to do way more than anybody should. You should never feel guilty for that."

"Yet how do you stop it when it's already there?" she asked defiantly. "Just because you tell me that I shouldn't feel guilty doesn't mean I can just wipe it away."

"No, of course not," she agreed. "You can't, and I get that. One of the hardest things to deal with is the constant failure we feel when we can't do something, and the joy when we can, but also realizing that you can't ever share those things with anybody is the worst," she added. "Believe me that this team does some pretty-amazing things, a lot of them. We see terrible things along the way, but we have each other, and that makes all the difference. You didn't have anybody, so the fact that you're even sane is huge. Yes, we've known people in our group and people we wanted to help who didn't have the capacity to handle it mentally, and that means they're in a place that we can't help them now. God knows we've tried. We check in on some of them to see if they've healed enough on the inside, but a lot of them just don't want anything to do with the current world. They just want to hide away and to stay away. We've tried many ways to get them to come back to reality, but they're not interested," Celia shared.

"That must be very hard too," Amy murmured. "I can't imagine what that's like for their families."

"For the families it's definitely very hard. It's hard for everybody, really. Yet what else are we to do? Life isn't always easy, but it is always a challenge. We do what we can do and hope for the best, no matter what we do."

Amy smiled at that. "I like that philosophy, and the fact that you have a team to provide support for everybody is huge. I'm just not so sure that it works for everyone."

"No, of course it doesn't work for all. It doesn't work for a lot of people a lot of the time, but, as our families have all grown and expanded, we've realized just how much our abilities have also grown and expanded. That leads me to ask you how or if anything changed when you had the car accident."

"Ah, yeah, the accident," she muttered.

"Was there one?" Celia asked.

"Oh, yeah, there definitely was one, and technically I died."

At that, Wallace squeezed her hand and sucked in his breath.

So, he didn't know. Amy nodded.

Wallace frowned at her. "You didn't tell me it was that bad."

"I didn't tell *anybody* it was that bad," she stated. "Remember how it's all about *not* letting too many people in. You are too many people, … all by yourself."

"Too bad," he muttered. "I was all-in before, and I'm still all-in now."

"And that's why, when I was kidnapped this time, … I was calling out for you," she shared, "because you were somebody I could telepathically communicate with at one time. So, it made sense that you might be somebody I could communicate with now."

He nodded and stayed quiet, watching as everybody else digested that.

"Okay, so one thing just came out right there," Terk noted. "You mentioned, when I was kidnapped *this time*. Can you explain that?"

She stared at him and then winced. "Yeah, I did say that, didn't I? Remember that child molester who got ahold of me long ago? Well, he really got ahold of me," she murmured. "I was kidnapped as his next victim, and, being a child, it was hard. Although thankfully I was too old for his sexual fantasies. At the ripe age of thirteen, fourteen maybe, I was well past what he preferred, but let's just say it was another one of those very traumatizing events in life that you don't ever want to repeat. When I got kidnapped this time, it was very different, a very different energy and a very different feel to these guys. Plus, I'm a whole lot older, and I'm not anywhere near as scared, terrorized, or whatever you want to call it, as I was back then. Back then I lived with the monsters in my head all the time. I knew what they were doing. I couldn't sleep for days or weeks on end," she shared, with a headshake, as she stared down at the empty coffee cup that she gripped tightly with both hands. She sighed, relaxed a bit, and added, "Now, that's all about me. What about you guys?"

Celia laughed. "Nice attempt to change the subject, and we'll let you because obviously what you described is still very painful. I want to be one of the first to tell you that I'm sorry. Not everybody is an asshole, and not all parents are assholes, even if they appear to be."

Amy laughed. "Yeah, that part about *appearing to be* was a problem for me. I learned to recognize the overt monsters, but I didn't learn to recognize the monsters in sheep's clothing. That would be the guys who kidnapped me this time. Not that they reminded me of my parents in any way, but …"

"When you have time to work on it," Celia suggested, "that inner child inside you needs some attention, some true healing. We have excellent healers here," she pointed out. "Believe me that any of us here would be more than willing to help." And, with that, Celia looked over at Terk. "I need to get back upstairs." She headed to the fridge, grabbed a jug of juice and a bottle of water and added, "We'll talk later." And, with that, she headed out of the room.

Wallace leaned over to Amy and whispered, "You handled that well."

She shrugged. "It didn't feel like it," she murmured, staring at him. "Seems as if opening up yourself is one of the hardest things to do."

"It's because you couldn't open yourself up that Jonas gave you a pass after your initial interview," Wallace shared. "I was rooting for you while talking to him about it, but he didn't figure you were team material."

She gave a half laugh. "He's probably right. I'm not team material, not *his team* material," she murmured. "I'm not sure I want anything to do with MI6, ... not when it's obvious that his team is as broken as any team I've ever seen."

"You mentioned how you didn't want anything to do with governments. Is anything personal in that?" Terk asked.

"Only in that it was always the local authorities pushing me to come help them, once they realized I could do something. Don't get me wrong. I don't blame them for that," she explained. "If you've got missing children, and you can't do anything, but you know somebody who can do something, who could potentially find answers, anyone would give in. I thoroughly understand and expect that part, but a couple individuals in power were ugly about it, and a couple weren't very understanding, and it just made me hesitant to deal with *any*, ... any government officials. But once my abilities came back stronger than ever, this little voice inside me was like, *Use it or lose it*, and I was okay with that—until the same little voice came back with this *Then you'll die* business. I don't have any way to explain that to you, but it felt very much as if I needed to do this in order to keep justifying my existence in some way, as if this is just part of my fate and what I have to do in this lifetime," she murmured. "I know that sounds horribly dramatic, and I don't mean it to be, but that is my reality."

"I think we all feel pretty much the same way here," Terk admitted, with a smile. "We all do what we do because we know that nobody else can."

"Exactly," she agreed, staring at him. "I hadn't considered it that way though."

"You need to spend some time just sorting yourself out," Terk suggested. "Think about what works, what doesn't work, what you want out of life, and realize you can have it. It's not a case of you get it once and then it's taken away or you get an offer and then it's gone. There's a lot in life you can have that I'm certain you haven't even considered as being on the table for you. But it is, and it's up to you to determine which way you want to make it all go."

"That sounds very simplistic and lovely," she replied, laughing. "But I think you and I both know it's not quite as easy as that."

"No, but you've made one brilliant choice," he pointed out. "For starters, you're here." At that, his phone rang. Terk looked down at it. "This is Jonas. Let me talk to him in private, and then I'll come back and set up a plan."

And, with that, he got up and walked out.

WALLACE, AMY, AND the rest of the off-duty team waited at the kitchen table for Terk to return. When he didn't, Wallace looked over at Amy and asked her, "Do you need a nap?"

She snorted. "I really was flagging, wasn't I?"

He nodded. "How about we go outside for a walk around?"

She hesitated, since most of the others had now left. "Do you think we're allowed?"

"We're absolutely allowed," he declared, with a smile. "Come on. Being outside for a bit will do you some good. You know, the fresh air and all." He had a goofy grin on his face.

They walked through the kitchen, waving at the people working away in the kitchen, as they headed outside.

Amy noted, "I think I counted four people at work in there."

Wallace noted, "You didn't eat much breakfast. Are you hungry now?"

"I was still on edge at breakfast," she murmured. "I'll make up for it at lunch."

He smiled at her. "There's no making up for missed meals. You know that, right?"

"Yeah, I know." As she got outside, she looked around and smiled. "Who would have thought anybody would have this castle all to themselves?" she murmured.

"Not exactly *to themselves*, as a lot of people live here."

"I only saw a fraction at breakfast, didn't I?"

"Absolutely. The rest? … Let's just say that a ton of other people live here, the team itself, their partners, their children."

"It must take an awful lot to run this place."

"Everybody helps," he said. "That's the joy of how it all works. Everybody has roles. Everybody has things to do. Everybody has something that they're involved in, usually something they like to do anyway," he added, nodding in agreement. "So, I don't think anybody has regrets or a problem being here. I think that, on a whole other level, it serves them all very well."

She smiled and nodded. "How could it not?" she whispered. "Even though it's huge, it's also warm and welcoming."

She determinedly put away her thoughts about how many people would be required to run this place. As soon as she saw the gardens, she cried out and walked over to the first set of rose bushes. "My God, these are heirloom roses."

"If you say so," Wallace muttered, with a shrug. "I can't

say I've ever had a chance to know the difference."

She looked up at him and smiled. "It's one of the things I buried myself in as I tried to heal," she shared. "Roses, all kinds of plants really. I'm still a novice in so many ways, but I absolutely adore them."

"I think they are therapeutic in their own way," he said, with a smile. "All we have to do is accept the healing they offer."

"Accepting healing is a very different story," she noted, turning to him. "We can all do only so much, and then, even though the water is running in our direction, or even flowing over us, you can't accept any more, and you need time to assimilate. It takes time to figure out what's going on."

He chuckled and held out his elbow, and she linked her arm with his. They walked through the gardens, and she couldn't help oohing and aahing over the many different varieties of flowers and plants. She looked at one area in astonishment. "How long have they been here?"

"Not really all that long I don't think," he noted, pointing out the mess ahead of them. "They've put a ton into getting the castle refurbed and getting the base operational. There's only so much money and energy for cleaning up the grounds."

"That makes sense," she replied, "but it's pretty spectacular out here already."

"I'm sure some enjoy it, yet probably others haven't even made it out here yet."

"I haven't seen the kids."

"You will," he declared cheerfully, "and there's a whole lot of them. I know that some of the apartments have their own kitchens and not everyone comes down to the big kitchen all that often. You appeared, so they chose to grace you with their presence." There was that smile of his again.

"Ooh, ouch," she said, with a laugh. "Not sure I want to be a novelty."

"Maybe, but in this place, slow assimilation is often better."

"I would think it's always better," she noted, "and it's been pretty easy so far."

"Good. So, when we go back inside, and twice as many people are there, you won't freak out, right?"

She glanced up at him and asked, "Really? Are there that many here?"

"I know of at least twenty-four, if not twenty-six people who live here. And I'm not privy to all the goings-on here. So could be twice that many, as far as I know. Hence the number of people working in the kitchen. They've got to feed them all."

She smiled. "You know a kitchen is one place I do not belong."

"You can't cook?" he asked.

"I can do mac and cheese." He winced, and she chuckled at the sight of his face all scrunched up. "What? Nobody likes mac and cheese?"

"Oh no, it's … it's an iconic food and all that, but, as far as being able to cook it, that's not exactly what I would consider cooking."

"I understand, which is why I said it," she stated, grinning at him. "I can manage simple meals, but not much more than that. I tend to catch things on fire." He stopped and looked down at her. She shrugged. "I think it's a special talent of mine."

"You want to explain that a little further?"

She shook her head. "No. Let's just say that I shouldn't

be left alone in the kitchen. I don't quite get how all of it works and how food is supposed to be cooked at a certain time, at a certain temperature. Everybody else manages to make it come out gorgeous, but me? Not so much. That's how I stay so skinny," she quipped, laughing. "My cooking is inedible."

They were still laughing and joking when they heard a shout from behind them. They turned to see Terk, walking toward them. She grinned up at him. "If you're hoping to put me to work in the kitchen, I was just telling Wallace here that I'll probably end up burning down the castle."

Terk smiled, then shook his head. "The good news is that castles don't burn easily. I gather you're not great at cooking."

"Nope, not at all," she admitted, looking around in circles. "Now, gardening, on the other hand, I love." She looked wistfully around her. "This is absolutely spectacular."

"It is," Terk agreed, "but I couldn't tell you one plant from another."

"I don't know all these varieties either, but a lot here are very special," she stated, "and you're blessed to have them."

"Blessed?" he asked in confusion.

"Yes," she confirmed. "Some of these are heirloom varieties, as in hundreds of years old. Some of them you can't even get anymore. You could almost set up a private grafting program, selling some of these offshore. I bet you could make a killing from this bunch."

"Anything that makes money I'm interested in," he stated, with a laugh. "This castle is bleeding us dry."

"Ah, I'm pretty sure that Jonas is paying a lot of those bills," Wallace pointed out, with a knowing smile.

"He is, and he'll pay again and then some," Terk replied,

with a note of satisfaction. "Just for your information, the young man you found in the tunnels is awake. He survived surgery just fine, and he's doing okay, considering. I've been told he very much wants to talk to both of you. I guess he didn't sleep well, worrying that you were still a victim and being tortured, as he had been."

"I would love to see him." Amy looked up at Wallace, and he nodded.

"I can take you in." He looked over at Terk. "And MI6 is okay with it, right?"

"They're hoping you can get more information out of him than they got."

"Of course they are," Wallace muttered, with a wry look. "Maybe we can. I don't know. I did talk to him initially, but he was in tough shape, so I want to see him doing a little bit better now." He looked around at Terk. "Are you good if we go in now?"

"I would suggest it," he replied, with a nod. "Jonas wants to meet you there and to talk to you as well."

"Okay, anything that we need a heads-up on?"

"He's hoping you guys can be convinced to help them find the guys who did this."

"Did he find the leak in his department?" Amy asked. "Because no point in us doing anything if it'll just go right back out to the kidnappers. We can't have them on our ass as soon as we go back in."

"Jonas thinks so. He had a new junior clerk on his staff who came forward yesterday and admitted that he might have inadvertently shared something."

She pondered that. "I'm not sure about the *inadvertently* part," she murmured. "That makes me very suspicious that the confession is also a setup."

Terk studied her for a long moment and smiled. "That was my first thought, so let's go find out."

"Are you coming too?" she asked.

"I thought I would, yeah. I want to see who this guy is and what's going on. Besides, Jonas and I have a little bit to talk about." And, with that, he headed toward the castle. "Let's take one of my rigs," he murmured.

"Are they bulletproof?" she asked, with spirit.

He grinned at her. "They absolutely are. Surely you can't burn that down too?"

"Only if it's got a cookstove in it."

Laughing, they headed back to the castle and the vehicle.

CHAPTER 7

A MY SAT IN the back seat of the beefed-up SUV the whole way into town, a trip that took over an hour. She dozed in and out as Terk and Wallace talked steadily in the front seat. Several times Wallace looked around at her.

She just smiled and waved him off. "I'm fine," she murmured.

When they finally pulled up to a stop, she jerked up and looked around to see what appeared to be government buildings. Leaning forward, a little more alert now, she noted, "I presume this is it, and it does seem vaguely familiar."

Terk nodded. "Yes, this is where Jonas wanted us to meet him."

"Good enough." And then she stopped for a moment, contemplated the situation, then eyed him curiously. "You do trust him, right?"

Terk smiled and nodded. "I do. There's always room and potential for people to change, but I've had no reason to doubt him in all these years that I've known him."

"Good enough," she replied. "I guess nobody's perfect, and nobody can stay perfect all the time. So … at least for the moment, he's not on my shit list."

At that, Wallace burst out laughing. "Glad to hear it. I am not surprised you have a shit list," he stated, still chuckling. "It might help if we knew who else was on it."

"As long as you're not on it," she quipped, tossing him a cheeky grin, "you're safe."

"But how will I know if I am or I'm not, if you don't tell me?"

"Ah, you'll have to just keep guessing, I suppose," she said, smirking, as she got out and stood beside Terk. "So, we're expecting him to be here, right?"

He nodded. "He will be. The question is whether something else is pulling him back and making him late." Just then Terk's phone rang. He answered it right away, "Yeah, Jonas. We're here. Where are you?" He looked around and nodded at something that Jonas shared. When Terk finally ended the call, he told them, "Jonas wants to meet us up in the offices. He's been held up with a phone call."

"Yet he was just talking to you," she pointed out.

He smiled. "Indeed, but now he has to make another call."

She rolled her eyes. "Typical bureaucracy for them. They would do and say anything to not have to get up from their desks."

Terk burst out laughing. "Personally I would rather be anywhere but at a desk."

"And yet look what you created for yourself," she pointed out in a teasing tone. "I don't imagine that you'll be getting out from behind that desk anytime soon."

"And here I was hoping I would have lots of people to take over various aspects of it," he stated, with a wry look in her direction. "When you start out with a company, you don't realize how quickly you scale up and what's required when you do."

"Oh, I agree, though I can't say it's anything I ever

thought I would go into."

"What, business?" he asked curiously.

She nodded. "Not that I had any idea for a business to run either."

"But I ran a team for the government," Terk explained, "so it just seemed to be a natural extension when we ended up going private."

"It is, and, besides, you're a caretaker."

At that, he frowned at her. "What the hell does that mean?"

She burst out laughing. "It sounded better than *running a rescue center*." He glared at her, but she didn't give in. "You know it yourself," she declared. "You collect people, people like me."

"Did I collect you?" he asked, with a wry tone. "Because, if I did, maybe I need to learn how to *uncollect* people."

"If you hadn't intended to, you wouldn't have thrown that signal out there, now would you?" She mentioned the beacon since he had failed to speak about it.

"It must have been a weak moment," Terk admitted. "Believe me that I got quite a few calls for me to reconsider that."

"Of course, and yet, as somebody who is benefiting from your assistance," she added, "I can't say that I'm against what you're doing."

"Of course not." He motioned with his hand, leading the way toward the front door. "That doesn't mean all this is something we want to continue."

"Yet, if you don't continue," she pointed out, "what else would you do?"

"I don't know. We all have families now, so we all have things that we want to consider, other than dealing with this crap on a regular basis."

"If you had enough money that you could all retire, you could look at that."

He shrugged. "That would be a lot of money."

"Yeah, but throwing a satellite into orbit, that's also a lot of money."

"Ah, you heard about that, did you?" He chuckled. "In our business it's mandatory."

"Sure, and I get that," she acknowledged, "but it always just seems that the bigger the boys, the more expensive the toys."

At that, he burst out laughing and nodded. "Very, very true." He looked over at Wallace and grinned. "You better watch out. She'll be quite a handful."

He smiled. "I know, but sometimes you really have no choice."

Terk studied the two of them for a long moment and then nodded. "That is very true. Now, let's figure out how to get you guys out of this, safe and sound."

"How do you make money off this?" Amy asked. "Because I'm not sure I have enough to pay you."

"You probably don't," Terk replied. "Who would? That's just the nature of the work, and it's incredibly expensive to run an operation like this. But a good share of the time we end up working in tandem with the government, and they can cover the cost."

"Does that work for you?" Amy asked.

"Sometimes it does and sometimes not," he said, sending her a smile. "In this case, you were kidnapped because of what happened at their offices, so the cost isn't on you. The cost is on them."

"That's a good thing," she muttered, with a heartfelt

sigh. "I was wondering, as I don't have a whole lot of options otherwise."

"We all have options," Terk declared, as he quickly led the way to the main entrance. "We just don't always know it."

Inside, she followed the men, looking back and realizing just what a different atmosphere it was today, versus when she'd been in to interview just a few days ago. Different building but same government. She shook her head, hating the sense of insecurity still gripping her. She moved closer to Wallace, as she grasped his hand. "Hope you don't mind, but I'm feeling a little bit like I've been here before, and it didn't have the greatest results."

He squeezed her hand gently. "I get that," he noted. "You'll be fine this time though."

"Sure, I will," she muttered, not at all convinced. "I just don't want to get separated from you guys again. That's when the sharp teeth come out."

Neither of them responded to that, and she looked over at Terk curiously. "Do you do much fieldwork?"

He shook his head. "Used to, but, no, not a lot since I started Guardian," he admitted. "I typically do if all of us are needed or if friends are involved," he added, with a clipped nod. "Unfortunately both happen a little too often."

As they walked through the building and headed to the elevators, she looked over at Terk. "Do you ever get some radar hit, a sense of something wrong?"

He nodded and, not even looking at her, asked in a low voice, "Are you getting something?"

She looked around and nodded earnestly. "I can't tell if I'm getting something or if it's just stuff brought on from the last time I met with MI6," she murmured. "That's why I was asking you."

He nodded. "It's always a good thing to double-check a situation because emotions can completely overrun your ability to detach," he explained. "At the moment I'm not getting anything, but it would be quite a coup for somebody to grab all three of us."

At that, Wallace sucked in his breath. "That's not a thought I want to contemplate. … Thank you for that mental image."

Terk shot him an amused glance. "Whatever senses you've got, turn them on—because you never quite know what's waiting for us."

"I guess that's why I was asking," Amy whispered, still glancing around nervously. "We really do trust that this will be okay, right?"

"I don't fully trust anything ever," Terk replied smoothly. "We do the best we can with what we have, with the expectation that it will all work out at some point," he shared. "We're not foolish about it, but we also realize that, in the world we live in and with the work that we do, things can happen. When things happen, they generally happen in a big ugly way in our world." He motioned forward and added, "What we're trying to do today is put a lot of that to the test."

Amy groaned. "I hear you. I just don't like anything about it right now."

He chuckled. "So far, not a whole lot you like about a lot of things."

"Ouch," she muttered. "That does make me sound like a prima donna, doesn't it?"

"I don't know about that, but it does make you wary, and, after what you've just been through, I think that's a good thing."

The elevator opened just then, and they stepped inside. Heads nodded in their direction, and a couple people just ignored them, as the elevator continued upward. She sent out a quick check to see if everything was okay in the world, as she could best figure it out. She wasn't getting any feedback, so she just shrugged. When they got off at the top, she looked over at Terk. "I'm still not getting anything," she whispered.

He nodded, as they stepped away from the others. "There's also a weird resonance in this building. I've never really understood why. Yet every time I've been here, something is dampening the energy, almost like a blocker was here." She stiffened, hearing that, and Terk nodded. "I don't think it's necessarily deliberate on their part, but—"

"And yet," Wallace interrupted, "if they could do that, it would be really smart."

Terk nodded. "Smart for them, not so great for us. We don't have a whole lot to go on here. However, when it comes to fighting some of these interesting characters in the world around us, the one thing I no longer trust is any government building, like this. You can never fully trust what you see or hear. What they're trying to do is disorient us."

"So, you do think it's deliberate then?" Amy asked in a low voice, as she looked around with a new awareness. "If Wallace and I were to join up with MI6, would we still be treated in the same way?"

Terk nodded, thinking it over. "Probably. You would potentially be on the inside for some of it, but to expect to be on the inside for all of it would be a bit of a stretch," he added. "In retrospect, after what the CIA did to us, their own team, I would suspect there would be some MI6 measures in place, in order to keep some information from you. What they don't realize is how much we can find out anyway. So essentially what it comes down to is that they're afraid of us, and anybody afraid of us is dangerous."

Wallace squeezed her hand. "He's not trying to scare you."

Terk looked at them. "Goodness no," he confirmed. "That's not what I was trying to do at all. However, remember that information is power, and it's critical that we share information on our side, so we understand what's going on. We must know what's happening around us, including the various allegiances at work as best we can," he shared in a calculated tone. "For want of a better phrase, I don't feel we're in danger at this moment. Yet I do recognize that it was not necessarily a good idea for me to come along on this trip."

"I gathered that much," Amy muttered, frowning.

"On the other hand, Jonas and I have a few things that we need to sort out, and he's come to my place many times. I figured this time, as a show of support and a willingness to trust our alliance, I would come here to just see what we were up against on this side, particularly after what happened to you," he said in concern, with a nod to Amy. "I've been working on a different kind of a defense system, and I just might get a chance to try it out today."

"Such as?" Amy asked, confused and curious.

"Something I'm calling *mind over matter* for now." Terk grinned.

"If you need our help, let us know," Wallace offered.

"Will do," Terk replied cheerfully. "Just remember that people who are afraid of us are dangerous, and people will always be afraid of us because they don't know what we can do, any more than we know exactly what we can do. As we're finding out at our place, what we could do before versus what we can do now is very, very different," he pointed out, "and, for that alone, we have to watch out."

And, with that, a door opened ahead of them, and Jonas stepped out. He lifted a hand in greeting. "There you are. I was afraid I would have to come down and find you guys."

"Nope, we're here," Amy replied.

He looked over at her and nodded. "You're looking much better."

"Better than what?" she asked, with a wry tone. "After all, I was kidnapped by somebody who got the information from your office."

He winced at that. "I was hoping we could get past that point."

"Oh, I'm sure we will," she stated, "but it's not very realistic to think it would happen today."

He snorted. "God, a comment like that puts you right in with this lot." He motioned his hand at Terk. "No wonder you're … Somehow something about all of you is so very similar to our guys."

Amy frowned. "And yet I would think most of us would feel that we're completely opposite of anybody here, not similar."

"Yeah, but still, for some of us on the outside, you have some very major similarities," he muttered. He motioned toward a room up ahead. "Come on. We're going in here, where we can get some privacy."

As they stepped inside, she looked around and asked, "When you say, *privacy*, what does that mean? Are we being recorded?"

He faced her and shook his head. "No way."

"Are we being watched?" she asked.

Again he shook his head.

She just nodded.

"Why?" he asked suspiciously, looking around. "Do you feel as if you are?"

"No, but it does feel odd, after visiting MI6 before, then being kidnapped as a direct result of my time with you," she noted. "It's made me very leery of your security here."

"And, for that, I'm sorry," he said sincerely, "and you're not wrong to feel that way. I'm just sorry it happened because of being interviewed by us."

"It certainly isn't how I wanted that experience to go. I understand I didn't make the cut anyway," she declared, with a note of amusement in her tone. "Then I knew that earlier."

Jonas flushed and raised both hands in mock surrender. "And yet apparently you're very good at what you do."

"I don't really even know what I can do," she admitted. "At least not anymore."

He didn't say anything to that but asked in a curious tone, "Would you consider working for us?"

She immediately shook her head.

"Why is that?" He frowned. "Also, that was a rather fast response."

"Because of what just happened," she replied, frowning at him in astonishment, unsure how he could not understand it. "If something sour is here and is big enough to allow such a thing to happen, why would I want anything to do with that?"

"And yet, if we fix it …"

"You'll have to in order to even continue to function

with any credibility," she stated. "I can't see how Terk or anyone like him would work with you after something like this. But personally, having already been burned by the mechanism in place—or lack of a mechanism—it would make me very leery to trust your group."

Jonas sighed. "It's kind of what I figured."

"So, it's a good thing I was written off anyway," she said, with a laugh.

He frowned at that. "It's not that you were written off," he clarified, "but we just … weren't exactly sure what to do with you."

"Of course not, and you were right to not be sure," she noted. "You need to go with your instincts too."

He glared at her. "That sounds suspiciously like something Terk would say."

She shrugged.

Jonas groaned, then faced Terk. "This has given my government a pause on their plans to set up such a team," he revealed. "So, their current thinking is that, if you're around and are willing to do work for us on an as-needed basis, it might be easier than trying to find our own team of psychics." He shrugged. "To be honest, it'll probably just delay the powers that be, while they try to find qualified people." He turned to Wallace. "What about you?"

"What about me?" Wallace asked, a note of amusement in his tone. "Do you really think that I would accept if she didn't?"

"What does she have to do with it?"

"I know what happened to her was because of a leak in your system," Wallace explained. "So that doesn't exactly promote confidence, you know?"

"Maybe not," Jonas muttered, "but we're not fools here

either. Surely we can fix what's gone wrong in our own house."

"That would be a great start," Amy interjected, "but the hotel staff may be involved too. In fact, all the hotels in the area are suspect as far as I'm concerned and should be part of your search for your moles."

"Moles?" Jonas repeated, frowning.

Amy nodded. "It's necessary if you plan to build such a team in the future."

He groaned at that and turned to Terk. "I know you wanted to talk to me and that they want to head to the hospital. I did have a few more questions for Amy," he added, as he looked at her in resignation, "if you've got another minute or two."

"You've got a minute or two," Amy confirmed, "but I definitely would rather be at the hospital than here. Yet I understand that this was a necessary stop along the way."

He smiled. "You mean, a necessary evil?"

She shrugged. "Hey, you called it, not me."

He laughed and proceeded to ask her a few more questions about the layout of the sewer area where she had been held captive, if her kidnappers had had any communication with the outside world that she overheard, or anything along that line. Every response was a flat-out no, as far as she was concerned.

"Remember that I was kept in a separate area. I didn't overhear whatever they were talking about, outside of the planned meetings with them or interactions with my guards. However, I definitely got the impression that they were looking at setting up a team like yours. I think it was because they had heard that you guys were doing that. So maybe you should put out the message that your plans have been canceled and let it filter through to them. Maybe they'll stop going after the people you interview."

Jonas sighed. "We have set up other protocols to address this issue."

She snorted. "Good, because that would really suck if these kidnappers grab somebody else. And it just adds to the fact that we need to get to the hospital and talk to that poor man as well."

"I would like to go along," Jonas added, "if that's okay with you. That's one of the reasons why I wanted you to come here first, so I could go in with you at the same time."

She shrugged. "That's fine, but we need to get going. I want to see that this poor guy is doing better and is protected, so he won't be a victim of these kidnappers again. Whether their victims have abilities or not, these kidnappers seem to be running out of patience. So far, I'm not so sure that the boss man running this whole kidnapping operation is terribly convinced that *anybody* has abilities. And that one egotistical bastard—Dominic—who fancied himself a mind reader? Well, maybe he was just a lot of bravado and inflated confidence, yet he clearly had something going on. So the boss man has maybe one psychic working for him. From what I saw of Dom though, I don't know that he'll maintain his presence in that criminal organization if he can't find others like him soon."

On that note, Jonas stepped away and made a couple arrangements by phone, then motioned at them. "Come on. Let's head out to the hospital. We'll take my rig."

She hesitated and looked over at Terk, but he was already shaking his head. "Nope, we'll take our own rig. Thanks for the offer though."

Jonas stared at him but eventually shrugged. He was

clearly not pleased with that. "Whatever," he muttered, then proceeded to lead the way out of the offices again.

As they went down the same elevator, she looked at him, still scrutinizing everything. "What kind of security do you even have here?"

"I would have said it was good security," he replied, "until this all happened."

"Yeah, it's always a bit of a blow when you find out things aren't quite as good as you would have hoped," she muttered. "On the other hand, I am wondering about the moles. Even though you mentioned how you found one person who may have been involved in an information leak, there could easily have been multiple people involved."

"And we are looking into that," Jonas replied, as he nodded in understanding. "What we can't control is what people do when they're out of the office. And just because they're working under a contract that requires they not speak and have even signed various legal documents to confirm that they don't, it doesn't necessarily keep people from doing just that. Particularly if they think they'll get money for it."

"Right," she muttered, "and money always seems to drive the criminal enterprise, doesn't it?"

"Exactly."

"Speaking of money, you never did tell me what you would offer me, just that very tempting range of salaries," she noted humorously. "But then I guess that's because you didn't get around to making the offer."

He looked at her and sighed. "You seem to be harping on that. Are you upset because you weren't offered a job?"

"No, I just feel as if I've been through enough, so it would have been nice to know what the wages for my skills would have been. Regardless I would still turn you down," she added, "but …"

"Would it make a difference?" he asked curiously.

She pondered that, then shrugged. "I don't know if it would or not, money being what it is. I still need to make a living, you know?"

He didn't say anything to address that. "Since the team itself isn't up and running, I wouldn't disclose that detail regarding money anyway," he shared. Yet he did glance over at Wallace. "However, if you ever want to talk, let me know."

Wallace snorted. "Right. So, I'm still on the docket, but she's not?"

Jonas shrugged. "After what she's been through, I don't blame her for not wanting anything to do with it," he conceded. "And maybe it's the same thing for you. I don't know, but it doesn't feel like it's the same thing."

"No, maybe not exactly the same, but still I have a certain level of uncertainty," he added cheerfully.

"So, in the meantime, you don't want to work for us, I suppose."

"Nope, not particularly," Wallace responded.

"If that's how it is, how about working for Terk?" Jonas asked.

"I'm not sure that Terk needs more people at this point, but, if he does, I would definitely consider that option."

"Why him and not me?" Jonas protested.

Terk chuckled but otherwise stayed silent.

Wallace replied, "For one thing, I understand where he's coming from and what he needs done. In your case it's the government," he noted, as if that explained away all his insecurities, "and that's kind of like operating in the dark all the time. It's not very comfortable for any of us."

"So what you're really saying is, you've got this problem with government again."

"Again?" he repeated, chuckling. "I think you'll find most of us do."

"Yep, that's exactly what we're finding. Most of you do, whether it's justified or not."

"Most of us would say it's fully justified, and most of us would say that anytime the government's involved, we have to watch out."

Jonas snorted. "But you do realize, while you *can* say that, it doesn't mean that anything is wrong with working for us."

"Other than the lack of transparency?" Amy added, with a smirk.

They were outside in the parking lot by now. She looked around and suggested, "Why don't we just meet you at the hospital?"

He nodded. "See you there in ten." He hopped into his vehicle as they walked over to theirs.

She looked between Wallace and Terk. "Anybody else get that weird feeling?"

Terk immediately nodded this time. "Yep."

Wallace asked, "But what was it?" He was clearly frustrated, more than any of them. "I got weird vibes off him, but I don't know what could be there."

"You really trust him?" she asked Terk again.

He nodded. "I do, and there's never been any reason not to. So far, it has all been in the clear."

"How about now though?" she asked, with a wry look. "I don't think even he's aware of it."

Wallace leaned forward and asked with suspicion in his tone, "Is he being tracked?"

"I think so," Terk stated. "I'm getting a weird buzz every time I'm around Jonas. Somehow we'll have to get a message to him and let him know that things aren't copacetic in his world, without triggering him to inadvertently pass that same information to whomever has bugged him."

"I can't imagine he'll be happy to find out that somebody got close enough to get the upper hand on him though," Amy noted.

"No, of course not, but he would still rather be free of that influence, instead of having to deal with whatever the hell's going on," Terk pointed out, looking at her. "When we work with somebody like that, we always try to give them the benefit of the doubt."

She muttered. "I might have trouble always being the better person."

"You're the better person until there's a reason not to be," Terk declared instantly. "When that happens, then there's a reason why, and we move on." They all piled in Terk's rig, as he drove them to the hospital. After he parked, he turned and nodded at them. "I presume you guys want to talk to the patient on your own."

"Yes," she confirmed. "And since you have a rapport with Jonas, you need to talk to him."

Terk nodded. "Yeah, I do. I just don't know that I want to do it the easy way."

"Because there is no *easy way* with him," Wallace stated, with a nod. "Telepathic communication is one thing, for those of us who at least have some idea of what the hell's going on. However, to work your way into somebody's cognitive senses when they haven't had any training—or worse, someone so skeptical as Jonas—that's a whole different story." Wallace smirked at Terk. "You could just write him a note instead."

"I was considering that," Terk admitted, with a sigh. "It's probably faster to do it that way, but it would be a lot more fun to scare the crap out of him."

With everybody still laughing, Wallace and Amy headed into the hospital, leaving Terk behind to catch up with Jonas. Once inside, the two walked toward the patient's room.

She asked Wallace, "What's his name?"

"It's Wallace as well, but that's his last name," he explained. "That was part of the confusion. It's Gerry Wallace, if I remember correctly."

"Poor man," she murmured.

As they got closer, they found a guard standing outside the room. As soon as Wallace identified himself and pulled out his ID, they were allowed to enter.

"I'm glad they're looking after him at least," Amy pointed out. "It seems he's been given the short end of the stick." As they stepped inside, the young man was sleeping. Hesitating at the doorway, she looked at Wallace. "Should we wake him?"

At that, the other man opened his eyes and stared at them. "Do I know you?" he asked in confusion.

She shook her head. "No, but this is the Wallace who you were mistaken for."

He studied Wallace, then nodded. "We have met then, but I don't remember much of that right now. We have a similar body type too."

"I was thinking that," Wallace added, as he walked closer. "I can't tell you how sorry I am."

"Yeah, well, I can't say I'm terribly impressed either. It's one thing to be punished for shit you've done, but another thing to be grabbed for somebody else's folly," he shared, with half a smile. "I'm Gerry Wallace, by the way."

"And I'm Wallace Cremayne," Wallace replied with a smile, as he reached out a hand. "How're you doing?"

He shrugged. "I'm not going anywhere soon," Gerry noted grimly, "but I'm out of that hellhole and alive, so believe me that I'm doing just fine." Gerry looked over at Amy. "So, if you are with Wallace, then you must be the woman those guys went after too."

She nodded. "Apparently."

"I'm sorry to hear that," Gerry muttered.

"Yeah, they got me too, but Wallace here rescued me."

At that, Gerry looked at Wallace and smiled. "It sounds as if you're the man of the hour then."

Wallace snorted. "I would have much preferred that there hadn't been any need for the two of you to be rescued in the first place."

Gerry's expression lost its humor, and he nodded. "I sure would like to get my hands on those men," he declared. "When I have the advantage, of course, not them. It's one thing to beat up somebody when they're drugged or restrained in some way, but it's hardly fair or sporting when two or three are against one, who didn't have a sporting chance to begin with," he pointed out, with a headshake. "Yet it does make you wonder what they're used to, … if this is the way they operate."

Amy grimaced. "I suspect they're used to taking advantage of people and taking what they want when they want it," she suggested. "Unfortunately you were in the wrong place at the wrong time."

"Story of my life," he said, with a cheerful glance in her direction. "Did they hurt you?" he asked in a sympathetic tone.

"They were getting ready to," she replied carefully. "They wanted to do some weird testing."

"Right?" he said, shaking his head. "Like what the hell was that all about? I don't know for sure, but they heard that I was in for a job interview with the government," Gerry offered. "And they seemed to think it was for some secret spy thing. They kept asking me what I knew and what would I do about this job offer," he added. "I couldn't figure that one out. I'd come to town for an interview and felt okay about it, but there had been no talk of any offer. I could use a job as much as the next guy, but I don't have anything to do with psychics or that sort of thing," he shared, with a headshake.

"I know, right? Who does?" she asked, with a snort. "Have you spoken to the government yet?"

"Yeah, I've had all kinds of police in here," he replied, "including government police, whatever the hell that means. At least as near as I could tell, MI5 was here, plus somebody else named Jonas was here earlier."

"Yeah, he's on his way up again," she noted. "We just spoke with him at his office."

Gerry rolled his eyes at that. "Good for you. I would just as soon stay well away from that sorry lot."

"Understood," she muttered, with a smile. She sat on the chair by the bed. "Look. I had a very different experience at their hands because I wasn't there very long, but I just wondered if you had any idea or overheard anything that would help us figure out who these guys were, what they were after, who they were working for, or anything along that line. I'm just afraid that they're not done and are planning on coming back after us."

At that, Gerry shifted in alarm. "They better not," he wailed. "Jesus, I hadn't even considered that." He stared at her and then shook his head frantically. "I'm a sitting duck in here. I really don't need them coming back after me."

"I'm not sure it's you that they would come back after, rather than Wallace here, but, in my case, the torture wasn't complete," she shared, with a grimace. "So, I don't know what it is that they were truly after, and I don't know what it'll take to get them off my case."

Gerry sat back slightly, relaxed a little more, and nodded. "That's quite true. They got rid of me fast. I couldn't even fake being psychic, if that's what they were looking for." He shrugged. "How does one even deal with that shit?" He looked over at Wallace. "If they haven't tried to recapture me yet," he suggested, "chances are they're really after you."

Wallace nodded. "Believe me that's on my mind."

"Yeah, it would be," Gerry confirmed, but with obvious relief he felt he was off the hook. He turned to Amy. "I don't know what to tell you about my experience with them. I felt lost most of the time that I actually remember, as if I wasn't cognitively aware of most of it." He shook his head. "I'm pretty sure I was drugged for a large portion of my *visit*. Then they kept asking me questions about something called remote viewing, plus ESP. and stuff like that," he shared, with a headshake. "That's not my field at all, so I don't know where they got the idea that they should even be talking to me about it. Of course they weren't talking to *me*. They thought they were talking to you." Gerry pointed to Wallace, with a nod. "Do you do any of that stuff?" he asked, looking at Wallace with suspicion and a mixture of fear.

Wallace shook his head. "No. There was talk within MI6 about setting up some remote viewing team, like they had in the Cold War," he explained, knowing he had to give something to get something here. "Yet I'm not sure how these kidnappers got hold of that information."

"One did talk to somebody on the phone."

"What was his name? The caller or the guy on the other end?"

Gerry pondered that for a moment. "I forgot until just now when you asked me that. They were talking about somebody having information, or at least some of the information shifting," he began, as he stared off in the distance. "I want to say, *Dominic,* but I don't know for sure." He closed his eyes in pain and shifted uneasily. "It was all pretty blurry."

"Any idea what the context was?" she asked, studying him closely. "Was it during a phone call, and your guard mentioned something like, *Okay, Dominic, thanks,* or was it more like, *Talk to Dominic* or ..."

"It was about Dominic bringing something—or more like he's found new information—something like that." Gerry shrugged. "Again, really not my thing, and, as I told you, I was pretty damn out of it."

Amy grinned. "You did great. I'm not sure it's really anybody's thing though," she clarified, with a smirk. "When you think about it, this group had caused a lot of headaches."

"Yeah, you're not kidding," Gerry yawned just then. "I really just want to go home."

"Where's home?" Wallace asked curiously.

"Brighton," he replied. "I want to go back to my mates and forget this ever happened. I wish I could tell them, but it's not as if they'll believe me anyway."

"You're probably better off not talking about it," Wallace suggested. "Not only will your friends probably not understand, but you don't want word getting back to these guys that you're talking about them and maybe could identify them."

Visibly paling and sinking back into the hospital bed, Gerry stared at him and swallowed hard, nodding several times. "That sounds like good advice. The last thing I want is these guys coming back, thinking that I ratted on them." He shook his head, then looked over at Amy. "They're really scary."

She nodded. "You're right. They aren't people I ever want to see again either."

Wallace reached out a hand and squeezed hers. "That's why we're here," he noted. "We're trying to figure out who these guys are and confirm they don't come back after any of us again. Not ever again."

"Yeah, well, I hope all you guys just lose my name and number," Gerry added. "I don't know whether you did something to attract their attention or not," he said, "but, from my point of view, it would be great if you could just keep me out of it."

Amy smiled. "You were never intended to be in it in the first place."

"Yeah, I know, but somehow that's not bringing me much comfort right now."

"Have you had any other visitors?" she asked curiously.

"No, and I haven't told anybody I'm here. I'm not sure anybody even knew I was missing, and I wasn't gone all that long, so they probably thought I was off on a bender." He sighed. "Believe me that I do want to go on a bender, but considering I was drinking at the pub when I was picked up by these lunatics, that's the last thing I feel like doing right now."

Amy nodded. "I agree and totally understand," she replied. "I can't say that would be anything I would want to go back to myself."

"Yeah, it might have been the last drinking binge I ever go on," Gerry noted, with feeling. "So, maybe something good came out of this after all."

Amy watched as Gerry was starting to look tired and worn down. So she got up to head out. "Thank you for speaking with us. I know you probably didn't want to, but you did. So, thanks for that."

He shrugged. "Yeah, well, if I remember anything else, I'll contact you."

At that, Wallace handed over his phone number. "If you do remember anything, please contact us. And, if you need anything, I'll be there. I really don't want to end up in their clutches, and I don't want Amy here to get caught up in it again either."

Gerry winced at that. "No, you do whatever it takes to avoid them. They're just *asshole enough* that I could see them torturing the both of you."

She nodded. "I didn't get the impression that they gave a shit about anybody except themselves, so, yeah, any information you can come up with would be a huge help." She gave Gerry a wave, stepped out into the hallway, looked at the guard, and asked, "Anybody else been here?"

He shook his head. "Just MI6."

"No MI5?"

He frowned at her, then shook his head. "No." His tone was not very friendly.

"Okay," she muttered. "I'm a little worried about his kidnappers coming back after him."

"And yet we aren't expecting it, are we?" the guard asked curiously. "The kidnappers seemingly got what they could from him and dumped him."

"That's our impression, but he just remembered a

name," she shared. "If the kidnappers find that out? … Well, all bets are off."

He looked back at the door to Gerry's hospital room.

When Wallace joined them, the guard added, "Poor bugger, it's one thing to get beat up for shit you did, but it's another to get beat up for somebody else's shit."

She smiled at him. "That's what we were just saying. It sucks to be him right now."

"Absolutely."

With a wave of her hand, she headed off toward the parking lot, Wallace right behind her. As they headed down the stairwell, he asked her in concern, "Are you okay?"

"I am," she replied, "but it still feels as if something's very wrong in all of this."

"Yeah, but what could be wrong here? Have you got a reason why that would be?"

She shook her head. "No, I don't, and that's the problem. … I feel as if I'm in a holding pattern, as if I'm just waiting for the kidnappers to come back after us. Nothing worse than that, you know?"

"Let's connect with Terk and see if he's got any information."

As they headed out to the parking lot, she looked around. "I see no sign of him."

Wallace nodded. "I'm not sure I would expect him to be waiting in the parking lot anyway."

She hesitated. "They wouldn't go after him, would they? The kidnappers?"

"If they were looking for a psychic? Maybe. But that would be one of the worst mistakes they could ever make."

"Maybe," she muttered, "but that doesn't mean that they aren't stupid enough to try it, particularly if they don't know who they are dealing with."

They walked over to Terk's rig to confirm that he wasn't in there, waiting for them. Wallace pulled out his phone. "Let me call Jonas, and we'll see where he's at."

Just as he went to make a phone call, somebody came up behind them. "Hey, you looking for Terk?"

She turned to look at the new arrival, as alarms went off in her mind. "Have you seen him?"

He just smiled at her. "Sure have." With that, he snatched her into his arms and injected a hypodermic needle into her shoulder.

She didn't even get a chance to cry out or to warn Wallace. In the dim recesses of her mind, she realized that several other men had quickly joined the first one and that this was a well-planned attack. The truth was, she and Wallace and Terk probably didn't have a chance right from the beginning. That was her last thought as she slowly sagged to the pavement, still in this man's arms, as he held her until she succumbed to the drugs.

Last thing she heard was, "Hurry up. We have to get them out of here fast."

Then darkness was all around her, and she heard nothing more.

WHATEVER THEY HAD sprayed in his face had knocked him out heavily, but Wallace was still struggling to get his mind wrapped around what had happened. They'd been taken so fast that he had no warning, and, for that, he blamed himself.

Amy had been saying that it didn't feel right, that something was going on. He struggled to clear the cobwebs out of his brain and yet not move, trying to sort out whether they were alone—or he was alone—and if Terk was taken as well. Wallace was not sure of anything at this point. If Terk had been taken as well, that would be an even worse scenario.

Although, with Terk's abilities, maybe they could get out of this that much faster. Wallace had never met anybody quite like Terk, who probably had talents that even he wasn't sure what to do with at this stage of his life. Didn't he just say at the beginning of this trip how he was working on a new psychic defense, whatever the hell that meant? Yet what Terk could do seemed endless. Still, surely he could suddenly come up against something he didn't even know about, and then what would Terk do? Sit there and look puzzled? The bigger question Wallace had was, how long would it take Terk to get them out of this mess?

Wallace opened his eyes a slit and looked around. He was alone in a room that had a mustiness to it, dark dankness all around, and he realized almost immediately that he was back down in the sewer tunnels. He swore at that.

It was much harder to get messages in and out down here, which was probably exactly why they were being held here. He'd barely had a chance to orient himself, when a door opened, and somebody walked in.

A snort filled the air. "If you're thinking to pass yourself off as still being knocked out, forget it," the man said in contempt. "I already saw you open your eyes."

Wallace opened his eyes and stared at the stranger. "What's this all about?" he asked, his tone mild, curious even.

"All kinds of things," he replied, with a light chuckle, "but, if you're smart, you'll pay attention and not do anything stupid."

Wallace just nodded at that because, well, that was the smart thing. It's just that he didn't tend to be a smart person when it came to being kidnapped and attacked. "You must have some reason for attacking us," he began. "Is she okay?"

"She is, for the moment. Beyond that, I don't have all the details," he replied, with a one-arm shrug. "The boss will talk to you when he's ready," he added. "I came to confirm that you understood that any resistance on your part could get a lot of people in trouble, and she'll be the one who'll get hurt."

Inside, Wallace felt his heart slam against his chest. Of course. That would make perfect sense. If they didn't think she had any abilities, then bringing her as leverage against him made a sick kind of sense. "That's nice," Wallace muttered. "Nice to know what I'm up against. You guys really have no boundaries, do you?"

"No, not when it comes to this shit," he stated. "This isn't my deal, but, if you guys can do even one-tenth of what they say, I would rather have you on our side than off it."

"This is how you get somebody on your side?" Wallace asked in astonishment. "You kidnap my girlfriend and threaten her to keep me obedient?"

"Until we know where things are at, it seems to be the safest bet," he said, with a snort. He tossed over a bottle of water. "That's to help you shake the drugs. Spray is effective, but it's shit on the face afterward." And, with that, he turned and left.

Wallace found that his eyes stung from whatever they had sprayed him with as well. He opened the water bottle, appreciating the fact that it was sealed, so it felt somewhat trustworthy, then took a long drink. He was still trying to process what these guys thought they were doing here, then realized it would be the same damn shit all over again.

They were looking for psychics and wanted to get somebody who was real, but whether they had Terk or not was something else altogether. Wallace hoped not. He mentally sent out a message to Terk, but, of course, being underground, as he'd found out before, it would be hard to get any messages in or out. Almost immediately though, he heard from Terk.

You awake? Terk asked.

I am. You?

I am.

So, you've been taken too? Wallace asked Terk.

Apparently, Terk replied, a resigned note in his tone. *I walked out to the rig to get my phone, which I'd left behind, and turned around to find somebody spraying shit in my face.*

Yeah, same here, Wallace shared. *What about Jonas?*

He's right here beside me.

Oh, crap, Wallace muttered.

Yeah, that just adds to it. And Amy?

I haven't seen her, but I believe they have her. They've threatened me with her.

In what way?

The telepathic connection was a little bit staticky, but at least it was communication, and Wallace would utilize it to his full advantage. *They would use her to keep me compliant.*

Right. So, they saw you together and figured out that you two were a couple, Terk noted. *Too bad she doesn't know that.*

I'm sure they're busy telling her that now, Wallace replied, *though she may not take it all that well.*

A note of laughter filled Terk's tone when he stated, *You might be surprised. What we need to do is figure out how many we've got and take any advantage to get out of here fast, including some psychic warfare.*

Wallace agreed. Terk was all about a clinical perception.

Terk added, *I really don't have time for this shit.*

You and me both, Wallace agreed, with laughter in his tone. *So, if you've got a plan, let me know what I'm supposed to do. I've only seen one person up until now.*

Me too, Terk confirmed, *but I heard something about the boss coming in a little bit.*

Yeah, not sure I trust any bosses at this point.

No, I don't either. I do know that Jonas will have one hell of a headache. He woke up spitting mad, so they knocked him out again.

Oh, great. Nice to know that violence is their modus operandi.

We already knew that though, Terk pointed out. *Whoever doesn't cooperate will end up in the tunnels, broken and battered, like Gerry Wallace.*

Right, Wallace muttered. *He's not part of this, is he?*

Terk stopped and assessed that question again. *I would think not,* he replied. *Getting his ass kicked to that degree wouldn't exactly engender someone to be a part of this.*

That's what I thought. It just was one of those random mental questions I get, Wallace shared, with a snort.

Keep them coming. We need to consider all avenues. Another thing to remember. I think Jonas recognized somebody from his office among our kidnappers.

That makes sense. We knew the kidnappers had to have somebody else on the inside, and Amy asked Jonas many times if he'd cleaned house. But his recognizing somebody is definitely a big problem for us. … The kidnappers won't keep Jonas alive, will they?

Terk went quiet for a long time. *It'll be hard to keep Jonas alive,* Terk stated. *As much as I want to think that these guys will be reasonable, when they find out they have one of the MI6 bosses here, reason will go out the window, and I don't think they're above using his presence to their advantage.*

And yet what do they want? Wallace asked. *I get it when they grabbed us, but taking on MI6 like that? … It's a whole different story.*

It is. It elevates things in a completely different way, so I'm operating on the premise that they didn't know who Jonas was.

But they do now, since Jonas recognized someone.

That'll be the game changer here, Terk noted. *And we'll have to see just what they think of that. It could very well be that they want to dispose of him first.*

I won't take that kindly, Wallace muttered. *I don't know Jonas very well, but—*

Don't worry, Terk said. *I do know him, very well, and I still won't let it happen.*

That speaks volumes. Wallace chuckled. *Any chance you can contact the rest of your team?*

Already mustered, he confirmed, *and they know roughly where we are, and they're heading toward us now.*

That's good news, Wallace replied. *I've also got wind of Riff being out here somewhere.*

Yeah, he's looking for us as well, Terk agreed, *and will likely get here before the others.*

Maybe, but he's still a bit of a wild card.

Riff? That's true in a way, I guess, Terk conceded, *but his heart's in the right place. His operational status is a little bit dodgy at times, but he manages it well.*

Meaning he's definitely a wild card, and you never quite know where he is.

Yep, that's exactly what I mean, Terk declared.

Just then Wallace's door opened, and he went quiet. Out loud, he asked the other guy, "Your boss here now?"

The guy stared at him suspiciously. "Were you talking to someone?"

"No, of course I wasn't talking. You see someone here? Who will I talk to? Myself? Although, if you're out there listening to me, that makes me feel creepy, you know? Sometimes people talk to themselves so they don't get too scared."

The other guy curled a lip. "If you're scared now, just wait until the boss gets here." And, with that cryptic comment, he slammed the door.

Wallace told Terk about it. *So, they have somebody, a receiver or whatever, who's picking up signals. I'm not even sure if it's a person or a tool.*

Oh, now that *I don't want to hear,* Terk grumbled. *I've been up against too many tools lately to make me happy.*

Right, but you also know that, wherever there is one set of abilities, other people are out there trying to steal them, to use them to their advantage or whatever, Wallace pointed out. *So, in this case, I can't say I would be terribly surprised.*

Maybe not, I just wouldn't want it to be this *case,* Terk clarified. *So we'll keep an open mind on it, and thanks for the heads-up. Looks as if I'm about to get company.* And, with that, Terk signed off.

Within minutes, Wallace's door opened again, and he stared at the same man from before.

He motioned at him. "Get up. The boss is here."

"Oh good," Wallace replied. "I would really appreciate clearing this up, so I can get the hell out of here."

"You ain't going nowhere," he muttered. "Neither is that

chick of yours."

He stiffened and glared at him. "Did you hurt her?"

"Nope, not yet, but I'm guessing it will go that way pretty fast. She's quite the mouthpiece."

"She's also been scared, kidnapped, rescued, and now kidnapped again," Wallace shared. "So I can't imagine she's feeling very cooperative right now."

"She shouldn't get into such shit then, should she?" the guard stated, with a sneer. "What the hell does she expect?"

After such a strange comment, and not having any answer or understanding of what this guy was after, Wallace fell silent. He was led into another room, and there was Terk, Jonas, and Amy. Amy bolted to her feet and raced over to him.

Knowing that these guys already assumed they were an item, he just held her close and whispered, "Looks as if you were right. Something was wrong."

CHAPTER 8

AMY LOOKED UP at him, teary-eyed, and asked, "They didn't hurt you?" He shook his head. "Good." She glared at the men around her. "Remember that I don't want you hurting him."

"Yeah, yeah, yeah," one of the men said sarcastically, with a sneer for good measure. "We're all very concerned about what you want right now."

She shrugged. "I get it. You don't give a shit about me at all," she declared. "The fact that I'm even back here in this nasty hellhole just pisses me off. What's the matter? You didn't like the fact that I escaped last time?"

"You wouldn't have escaped if we hadn't let you," stated one of the guards. "So just shut up and sit down while we wait."

She sat down beside Wallace, her gaze on Terk, but her gaze was so obvious and so intense that Wallace nudged her. When she turned to face him, he gave her the tiniest headshake. She sat back and waited.

"You guys still didn't tell us what you're after," Wallace noted.

"No, and I also told you not to talk, as you'll find out soon enough. Why can't you be like this guy here and just be quiet?" asked one of the three men facing them.

The door opened without warning, and she jolted. One

of the men gave her a smirk, as if to say she was in for it now. She stiffened when she saw the same arrogant guy from before. "So, it is you again." She groaned, staring at him with animosity. "What's the matter, Dominic? Can't leave me alone?"

"I want to," he declared, with a hard glance her way, "but you keep getting in my way."

"Then just let me go," she said instantly. "I'm not part of this, so just let me go."

"We grabbed the wrong guy before, and now we have the right guy. Knowing that you won't exactly cooperate, we've decided to keep you as part of the group."

"*Lovely*," she muttered.

He gave her a fat smile. "On the other hand, if you're nice, you might survive this."

She glared at him. "Yet I'm hearing a *maybe*, as in a very slim chance of that happening,"

He shrugged. "You told me that you didn't have anything to do with this guy."

"I didn't tell you any such thing," she declared in astonishment. "You didn't even ask." He glared at her, and she shrugged. "If you can't ask the right questions, how am I supposed to know what you want?"

He stared at her for a long moment. "I would be quite happy to just smack that look off your face," he began, with a stern gaze. "But I happen to know that people want things right now, and they'll want them from you too. So, we'll just hold off on that for the time being."

"I've noticed you're not quite so cocky or arrogant this time. What happened, *Dom*? Did you get in trouble for my leaving?"

"You weren't supposed to leave. We didn't release you to go."

She stared at him. "Hang on a minute. Are you telling me that I'm not allowed to do anything but what you tell me to do?"

"Exactly," he confirmed. "Too bad you didn't get that message the first time."

"Even if I got the message, why on earth would you think that anybody who's been kidnapped and held against their will would play by those rules?"

"If you want to stay alive," Dom stated, glaring at her, "that's what you should do. Of course, if you don't give a shit about staying alive, that's a whole different story. However, I presume you do care about these people and keeping them alive?"

Her jaw dropped. "So, I'm here to be tortured so you can get information from these guys?" she asked, her voice faint. "That's how Machiavellian you guys are?"

He glared at her. "I don't even know what the hell that means, and I don't really give a damn. I don't need to be dealing with whatever you're spouting," he hissed. "What I want is answers."

"Sure," she muttered. "Fly at it."

Dom nodded. "I figured you would probably be a little more cooperative as long as you were with him."

She nodded. "That's possible," she muttered. "I probably feel a little calmer around him."

He nodded. "Yeah, that's to be expected, you being female and all."

She stiffened, but Wallace gripped her hand.

Meanwhile, Dom turned his attention to Jonas, who sat quietly off to the side. His lip curled even more. "Now, what to do with you, now that we've got you," he muttered. "That's a problem."

Jonas nodded. "It sure the fuck is," he stated, his tone low and deadly.

She stared at him, really quite delighted at Jonas's response.

Dom laughed hysterically. "Threats, threats, threats," he muttered in a mock tone. "I really don't give a shit. I get it. You're upset and pissed off. Whatever. Just deal with it. We have the upper hand right now. That's what counts."

"Is that *all* that counts though?" she asked, staring at Dom. "Surely there's more to life than that."

"There probably is, but, if people like you would just shut up and would just get out of my face about it, I could get on with what I need to do."

"When's the big boss coming?" Amy asked, smiling. Dom glared at her, and she shrugged. "He was here last time. Did you get in trouble?"

Dom turned his attention to Jonas. "I could shut her up, you know?" Dom began. "She won't like it, and I really hate women's tears and the screams. Jesus, they always make it sound as if you just beat the complete crap out of them, when all you did was pop them because they needed it."

Amy stiffened at that, but, with Wallace patting her hand, she realized Dom was probably just trying to get a rise out of her. As she watched the interaction between Dom and Jonas, she realized something else was going on here. "You two seem to know each other," Amy noted. "Is he one of the assholes who works for you?"

Jonas shook his head. "No, I was wondering about hiring him for the same job that I had been looking at you for, but I figured he was too unstable."

At that, Dom glared at him. "Like hell."

"So you know him as Dominic too, right?" she suddenly

asked Jonas.

Dom glared at her.

Amy muttered, "Oh, right. I'm just supposed to shut up, aren't I?" She chuckled.

"Yeah, too late," he muttered. "Believe me that I'm counting every one of the mistakes you make right now, and I'll be sure that you pay for them. All of them."

She stared at him. "I'll pay for something when I don't even know what I did?"

"Remember that part about shutting up? Any chance you could try that? Even just for a minute for the sake of my sanity?" Dom asked.

She shrugged. "Oh, I can try, but I can't help but wonder, when you two clearly know each other and when clearly something is going on between the two of you." She considered Dom for a long moment. "Since you've kidnapped me twice now, I really want to know what's going on."

"Nothing's going on. We got wind of MI6 creating a new team, so I applied. That way I could get the details on what they were looking for—and not get accepted," he said, with a laugh. "They can use whatever excuse they want for that," he added, "but I know the truth."

"Yeah, you're too unstable," Amy declared, with a nod. "Anybody can see that."

Dom sucked in his breath and stared at her. "Have you got a death wish?"

"Nope. You know what I do have?" she replied. "I have a really short temper when it comes to assholes like you, kidnapping me a second time, and then planning to use me as a bargaining chip," she muttered.

"If you had anybody decent looking after you, they would have protected you."

"Looking after me?" she repeated, stiffening and glaring at him. "Is that kind of like needing a keeper? As if I can't look after myself?"

"I would say, from the looks of it, you really can't look after yourself, now can you?" Dom asked, with a sneer. "You do see where you are for the second time?"

She slumped back in place. "Good point," she muttered.

He burst out laughing. "If you weren't so damn ugly, I might think about keeping you around."

She snorted. "Wow, just when I think that maybe something human is inside you, you go and open your mouth again, and some other shit pops out."

He stared at her. "You do realize that I can have you killed at any moment."

"You do realize that I can die at any moment, regardless, right? Just walking around here in this toxic sludge is likely to get me killed, particularly after I've spent however long down in this unhealthy piss-hole," she said, glaring at her surroundings. "You guys really know how to show a girl a good time."

"If you want a good time," Dom whispered, his voice dropping in a threatening tone, "I'll let the men have you."

"Yeah?" she asked, daring him. "You and how many others?"

He stared at her in shock.

Getting a telepathic message from Terk, she gave a slight nod at his suggestion. She wondered why Terk had been so silent up until now. She smirked at Dom. "You have no fucking idea what you're up against, and I'm getting really tired of your shit."

Dom stared at her, then shook his head. "I'm pretty sure that bravado of yours is all a bluff," Dom replied, "but I have to tell you, you're working that angle pretty well."

"*Uh-huh*," she murmured, staring at him. "You've got no idea what I've got working." And, with that, she settled back. "Now, if you have your threats over with, I need water."

"I don't give a shit what you need."

She glared at him and repeated, "I need water."

He groaned and bellowed, "Could somebody please get the diva a bottle of water?"

Almost instantly a bottle was placed beside her. She popped the cap and took a long swig. Then she handed it to Wallace. "You need some?"

He nodded and took a swig, then handed it over to Terk. Terk had a drink and then handed it to Jonas. By the time Jonas had a drink, the water was gone.

"That looks to be have been completely choreographed, planned, sharing that drink," Dom pointed out. "What the hell?"

"Or maybe we are all just thirsty, you idiot," Amy replied. "You might try using some common sense as you try to convince everyone how psychic you are."

Terk added in a calm voice, "We're just trying to be cooperative."

"Yeah, *right*," Dom grumbled, red-faced now and turning to confront Amy.

Then the door to this room opened. The same boss man walked in that she had seen the last time. She smiled. "There you are. I wondered when you would show up."

He frowned at her, saw the other three captives, then turned to look at his minions. "This again?" he asked.

"Haven't had a chance to get started yet," Dom said to Burly.

But Dom's demeanor did change, as if somewhere along the line he'd taken a couple of dressing downs, which she was glad to see, but it also meant that the boss had more control over Dom than she'd expected, and that wasn't good. Certain things she was okay with, but surprises like that were never good.

Dom looked over at her and smiled. "See? Now you'll be in trouble."

She stared at him in amazement, shaking her head. "Just like a two-year-old. Blows me away."

Burly stared at her, then asked Dominic, "What's going on?"

When Dom wouldn't reply, Amy interjected, "Dom got in trouble with you, didn't he?"

Burly laughed. "Very true, but so are you. You had no right to leave, but you went ahead and did just that."

"I had every right," Amy declared. "You kidnapped me and held me against my will, so of course I had the right to leave. That's how it works. You, as the kidnapper, try to force me to stay. I, as the prisoner, try to get the hell away."

Burly blinked. "It's not as if there are any rules to this."

"There sure as hell are," Amy argued. "It's a rule of nature between predator and prey. You can't get mad at me for self-preservation."

Burly shrugged. "You do have a point." He turned back to Dominic and the others. "You are now picking up MI6 agents?" he asked, walking over to stare first at Terk and then at Jonas. "And your reason for that?"

"Because they're idiots," Amy shared.

Burly turned that gaze on her, and she wondered if she'd finally pushed it too far.

"You've got a mouth on you, that's for sure," Burly noted, "but you might want to watch it before I decide you're too much trouble."

She felt Wallace squeezing her hand in warning. She smiled up at the boss. "Maybe so," she conceded, "but, if you're just here to kill us anyway, what difference does it make?"

"Why would I kill you?" he asked, looking at her curiously.

"Considering what you did to that poor man in the hospital, that seems to be your MO when people don't *cooperate.*"

He frowned at her, then turned to his minions again. "He survived?"

They all nodded.

"That does not make me happy," Burly muttered.

"*Right,*" Amy noted, "so the poor guy wasn't even intended to survive."

"No, he really wasn't," Burly admitted. "We'll have to take care of that now too." He turned and looked at Dom. "That is another one of your fuckups that you'll have to *unfuck.* Where is he now?"

One of his minions shared, "He's still in the hospital, and he'll be there for a while."

"Arrange for him to have an accident," Burly suggested. "Better make it a sudden embolism or something," he added, with a wave of his hand. "If the local authorities have already talked to him, I really don't want him out there spouting off more shit," he explained.

Immediately she felt bad for having mentioned it. Chances were, Gerry would find out soon enough, but now she wanted to warn everybody about what would happen next.

The boss looked over at Jonas. "So, Dominic here has some vendetta against you. Apparently you turned him down for the same job that I hired him for."

"That's because he's unstable," Jonas repeated. "I work for the government. You know as well as I do that stability is important."

"Sure it is," Burley agreed, "but instability allows you to do more things, to use them in better ways, special ways."

"It does, but there are consequences when you work for the government."

"Something I'm not too bothered about," Burly muttered, with a laugh. "I can do far more without the government holding us back. You should be happy that I'll at least carry on your wishes and find others like him to hold a team together," he added. "I'm sorry that didn't work out for you guys. It would have been fun to watch you struggle but crash and burn."

"What makes you think it didn't work out?" Jonas asked curiously.

"I heard it was canceled," Burly stated, studying him.

"Your information is wrong. Obviously we've had to change a few things," Jonas conceded, with a shrug, "but we're still going ahead."

"That is, if you can find anybody."

"That's always the challenge, and, of course, we need *stable* people," he repeated for a third time, nodding at Dominic.

Dom glared at him. "I'm perfectly stable, asshole," he snarled. "You just didn't want genius."

"And obviously your nose is still out of joint," the boss noted, turning to give him a hard look. "I don't want any personal vendettas here."

"Of course not, but what was I to do. Leave him there? He was talking with this guy." Dom waved a hand at Terk.

At that, the boss faced Terk and frowned. "Do I know you?"

Terk shrugged. "I have no idea, but I don't know you."

"Right, that makes sense. Who are you?" Terk gave his name, and the other man shrugged. "Don't know the name. Why were you there?"

"Because Amy's a friend of mine, and, after what she was put through, I offered her a place to recuperate. Just a favor for old times' sake."

"Ah," Burly replied, "a good Samaritan. You haven't figured out that being a good person results in getting your ass kicked, *huh*? Maybe you will after this. That is, if you survive."

Terk didn't say anything right away, watching Burly closely, then spoke. "What is it you're planning on doing with a team of psychics?" he asked curiously. "That's been done before."

"It's been done before, just not successfully," the boss clarified. "I plan to change that."

"It's hard to do if you don't have stable team members," Terk pointed out.

At that, the boss turned once again to look back at Dominic. "So I hear—repeatedly," Burly muttered, "and it's something I'll keep in mind."

Amy tried to hide her smirk, tried to keep from telepathically sharing the *Gotcha* reverberating in her mind. Burly's words gave the impression that, if Dominic became a problem, he would be disposed of.

Burly shrugged in response to Terk's point. "You're right. It has been done before and with some varying degrees of success, but, where there's a will, there's a way, and I'm certainly getting word about some teams who have had the right abilities," he shared. "I think it's just a matter of finding who can do what."

"Could be," Terk agreed, with a nod. "I don't imagine finding that out is an easy job. How do you test them? How do you figure out who's telling the truth and who's just full of shit?" he asked, as he nodded toward Dominic.

The boss laughed. "You guys really don't like Dom, do you?"

Amy snorted. "He is responsible for my being here twice now."

At that, the boss laughed again. "Good point. We actually wanted Wallace." He turned and looked at him. "So, sorry, bud, you're it."

Wallace stared at Burly. "Why do you want me?"

"You were heading for the same interview, were you not?"

"Sure, I was, and, like Amy here, I also didn't pass."

He turned and looked at Jonas. "Why not?"

"Same thing," Jonas muttered. "I need people who are stable."

The boss looked over at Wallace. "Interesting. So what's your story that renders you so unstable?"

"One of the requirements is no family, no friends, making sure that you can go out and get your ass kicked and not give a shit," he replied, staring at him. "That tends to be a problem for a lot of people. Plus, when I get asked questions about my personal and private life, I tend to tell people to shut the fuck up. Job interviews don't go so well after that, you know?"

Burly laughed. "I can't believe it was actually a job interview."

"No, not a job interview, more of a discussion in advance of something possibly happening," Wallace pointed out. "They hadn't got the paperwork together, and he was just starting to do the groundwork for it. But he couldn't make a case for the government if he didn't have people identified that he could potentially utilize. So, he was attempting to get together a list of people who might be willing."

"Would you be willing?" Burly asked.

"Not really, because it seems the reason why people want psychics is … *suspect*," he explained, "for lack of a better word."

"Meaning you have morals, and you don't want to be pushed into going against them?"

"Exactly," Wallace replied.

Burly smiled. "The good news is, … if you have abilities, I'm interested. The bad news is, if you have abilities and don't want to utilize them on my team, I have no problem keeping her to ensure you behave yourself."

At that, she stiffened. "That shit again," she muttered.

He nodded. "Yep, that shit again. What does matter is making sure that people are obedient, and, for me, loyalty is everything." He gave a sideways glance to Dom. "I can handle some instability, as long as the loyalty is there. The minute the loyalty is in question, then you have nothing." He turned and looked at Jonas. "I'm sure you would agree with that."

Jonas nodded. "Yep, which is why, as soon as I get out of here, I'll find the mole you have successfully used to follow whatever we're doing."

"I wouldn't worry about that one," Burly said. "I can't use him now, so I might as well put him away."

"Put him away?" she cried out in shock. "You'll just kill somebody?"

"Is that what I said?" Burly asked, deflecting.

"Yes, more or less," she declared, staring at him.

He shrugged. "Well then, yes, more or less, that's what I'll do. I do have to maintain a certain level of secrecy, you know?"

She didn't like hearing that at all.

Burly looked back at his men. "Separate them," he ordered. "I want to talk to Jonas privately, and then I'll have a conversation with Wallace," he shared, with a smile directed at him. "After that, we'll see how cooperative everybody is as to what comes next." He glared at Amy, as she stood up.

"If you hurt him," she stated cheerfully, "I won't help you at all."

He laughed. "Do you really think that's anything to threaten me with?"

"I don't know," she admitted, "but you seem to want a lot of *cooperation* from this new team. How can you even begin to think that a team with gifts and morals would work under coercion? You would have to watch your back all the time," she pointed out, with a headshake. "Is that really what you want?"

He just glared at her.

She sighed. "I've heard of some pretty stupid things in my life, but this one takes the cake."

Burly snapped, "Don't you ever shut up?"

She shrugged, looked back at Wallace, gave him a three-finger wave, and faced Burly once more. "Don't forget about me." She was taunting him, poking the bear, and it seemed to be working just fine. She gave a sly smirk in Terk's direction.

And, with that, she was gone.

WALLACE STARED AT the new room he had been led into. It amazed him that this many "clean" rooms were down here. Yet no doubt they were still in the sewer system, and it wasn't exactly a room. It was more of a space, a half hallway. He sat down on the single chair waiting for him, knowing that an interrogation was coming.

But he could really do or say only so much, and absolutely none of it would go the way Burly wanted. Wallace couldn't afford that to happen either. This was way past delicate subject matter. This was stuff that nobody should be allowed to even begin to think about. Whether the boss man wanted his own team of psychics or not, he would have to find people who were willing, and Amy had pointed out the big fly in the ointment.

You couldn't coerce a team. Maybe one individual. But a whole team of energy workers? No, the team had to be willing. They had to be on board every step of the way, particularly a gifted team like this. If you brought in psychics, you would have shit going on all over the place.

Wallace smiled at that concept because people just didn't realize what it was like to have psychics all around you. They knew everything. It didn't matter what you shared with them at first, the psychics would know if something else was going on, would know if some other process was ongoing that they weren't privy to, would know of other plans that involved them but which they hadn't been informed of. Then heads would roll—figuratively. Kinda like what Terk and Wallace and Amy were already doing, hoping to mess with their kidnappers' minds.

The boss man would end up with a hell of a shit show in

no time. As far as Wallace was concerned, Jonas was completely correct in reading Dominic as being unstable. Lots of psychics were, unfortunately. Terk seemed to do a decent job of weeding them out, but then he had a lot of people on board who could help him with that. Everybody had impressions and insider information, but, when it came to energy-worker stuff, it was all about instincts and being able to read energy. Lots of people on Terk's team could see that energy.

Wallace didn't need any looking glass to realize that Dominic was completely unstable. Wallace saw his aura, saw the unsteady wavelengths as they shimmered around Dom. He was probably quite talented, but he'd crossed the line into something bizarre in the meantime, and that would be what took him down.

Unfortunately Wallace didn't want anything to do with hurting another psychic, but, if it came to that, there would be no choice. He watched and waited, and finally the boss man walked in, a disgruntled look on his face.

"I guess that didn't go the way you wanted it to," Wallace noted.

"No, it sure didn't." Burly glared at him. "Let's hope the meeting with you goes better."

Wallace shrugged. "No guarantees."

"I'm totally serious and will beat the shit out of her," Burly declared, "particularly on a day like today, when I'm not getting what I need from people all around."

"What is it that you need?" Wallace asked curiously. "I don't quite understand the draw for a team like this in the first place. I could possibly see it—if a group of people were good friends with you, people you could trust—but psychics aren't exactly anything you want to play around with."

"That's exactly what I want to do," he stated defiantly. "I want a team that's solid and competent."

"It's not as if you can just put out an advertisement ..." Thinking about what Terk had done, he added, "Or set up an alert and have qualified people just show up."

Burly shrugged. "I'm not sure what other options there are because that's what I need. Now, back to you. Do you have any talent or not?"

"Some," he admitted, "but not necessarily anything you can utilize."

"I can utilize anything," Burly declared, staring at him with interest.

"I can see auras, no big deal," he shared, "and I'm a precog. In a way, I get some intuitive abilities when things are about to happen, but it's not as if you can train for this or can rely on this. It's not something where you can say, *Do it now*. It comes and goes."

Burly stared at him. "I did hear that happens sometimes."

"Absolutely."

"Don't you think it's something that would develop over time?"

"Maybe, but I'm not exactly young anymore, so I highly doubt that my abilities will change at this point."

"Then why would MI6 consider you?"

Wallace shrugged. "Hard to find people like us, qualified and gifted."

"So why do you think you didn't make the cut for the MI6 team?"

"Because frankly, I didn't like the intrusive questions, and I generally don't like leadership in the first place," he said, smirking. "I don't handle it well when people tell me what to do, and I definitely don't handle threats well," he added, giving Burly a hard look. "I have no intention of utilizing any ability for shit jobs. I've been asked to do that before, and the answer's always been no."

"Interesting," Burly murmured. "Why is it that the psychics I'm finding all seem to have some moral code?"

"It goes along with the job," Wallace stated, "which is more evidence that Dominic isn't truly psychic and is unstable. He'll do anything for a dollar, and, sure, you'll always get people like that, but is that really who you want, or do you just want people out there because they can do shit? Dom may also be out for your job, if he sees that it suits him or pays better."

"Dominic, I can handle. As to your other question, I want both, people with gifts who can be bought," he declared. "At least if they're driven by money, I know how to control them, because if they're not, it's pretty hard to get them to do anything you want them to do."

"Exactly. That's the problem with psychics, true psychics. You can get some who know some things some of the time, but it's not as if it's ever anything you can count on. Some psychics out there can predict an earthquake, but, just because they can predict it once, that doesn't mean that they'll predict it every other time. Other psychics have other areas where their predictions are focused. In other words, psychics are specialized. If it were that simple to find us, teams of people all over the world would be doing this shit."

At that, the boss man stared out into the distance.

Wallace continued. "I understand that's not what you want to hear," he added, "but you also have to counter whatever we're telling you with Dominic's chatter."

"Dominic has been telling me a lot, but I have also done

quite a bit of research. The CIA did a lot of remote viewing, and I've heard of healers who can do all kinds of stuff," Burly shared. "We will need healers because, if we'll be doing this work, then, chances are, we'll need to have them on hand as well."

"Do you have anybody yet?"

"I've just started this process," Burly shared, "and I have to admit it's not going the way I wanted it to."

"That's because you're using brute force. If you could find real psychics who want to do what you're doing for large sums of money, that's a different story, but to do it because they're forced to? … I can't imagine that their abilities would even work."

At that, the boss glared at him. "You need to explain that."

"Abilities are based on our senses being calm, centered, and balanced," Wallace clarified. "So, threats won't make them work at all. People will give you information, but that doesn't mean it'll be honest and real. It's more likely to be whatever you need, based on your orders. So, they may sometimes give you bad info just to get you off their backs," he added. "That'll be your problem with Dominic."

"It already is a problem with Dominic," he snapped. "I just don't want to believe that he's as unstable as you guys are making him out to be."

"I'm not sure how unstable he is, but definitely something is wrong there," Wallace pointed out. "Something odd, something that I wouldn't want to work with. *Ever.*"

"If Dominic wasn't in the picture, would you work with me?"

"No, because the work that you want to do isn't work that I want to do," Wallace stated.

"You don't know anything about the work I'm doing."

"No, but you used force to get me here. You kidnapped and threatened my girlfriend's life in order to keep me in line. So already I know you don't care about human life and free will. So there is absolutely no work that you will be doing that will fit into my ethical and moral code."

"If ethics weren't involved?" he asked, staring at him intently.

"That's a problem for me. Ethics are always involved."

"So then why is the thought that I might just kill her not enough to keep you in line?" he asked, puzzled. And it seemed as if he was sincerely asking.

"Because, at some point in time, every prisoner revolts," Wallace replied. "*Everyone*. They can only handle so much, and there always—and I mean *always*—comes a point where they will break. That's exactly what will happen," he stated. "So, you're better off to find willing psychics, maybe someone over in Russia or in third-world countries, where people don't have as many opportunities to go out in the world and won't have a clue about true freedom, maybe are used to having somebody like you as their leader."

"How do you find people like that?" Burly asked, a curious note in his tone.

Wallace stared at him, nonplussed. "A bunch of gangs are out there in the world. I don't know that they're worth contacting, but it would be a place to start."

He nodded absentmindedly. "I'll think about it." He got up and headed to the doorway. "Don't make any plans to leave anytime soon."

Wallace frowned at him. "At the moment, you've got all your henchmen here, all that I know about anyway. Five of you to guard the four of us. You've already threatened to kill a man you put in the hospital, who did absolutely nothing but be in the wrong place at the wrong time. Plus, you've threatened to kill my girlfriend. What is it you think I'll do?"

"I don't know," he muttered. "I'll have to give this some more thought."

And, with that, he turned and walked out.

CHAPTER 9

O NCE AGAIN, AMY was caught by the arm and dragged out into the larger room. There she saw Terk and Wallace. She shrugged off the arm holding her and glared at her guard, then walked over to sit down beside Wallace. "You guys get a better welcome than I did?"

"I did," Wallace replied cheerfully.

"Of course," she muttered. "I'm just the bait."

He leaned over, wrapped an arm around her, and gave her a hug. "But one hell of a cute *bait*," he muttered, chuckling slightly at her frustration.

She groaned. "Glad you're in a cheerful mood." He just smiled and kept his arm around her. She could tell that the atmosphere was crackling, and that something had shifted, but she didn't know what for sure. She looked over at Terk curiously, but he had a bland look on his face, not giving away a thing, but it was easy to see that something was afoot. She wanted to ask if their plan to plant seeds in the minds of these bad guys had taken root. Yet she had to remember that a receiver could be among those very bad guys.

Just then Wallace, as if realizing that she was struggling to keep her mouth shut, gave her a gentle squeeze, and whispered, "It's all fine."

And it felt fine; she just didn't know why or how. She glanced around in confusion, wondering what had changed.

Her guard joined the other two guards here, who seemed cheerful, laughing even. They made coffee and sat here, presumably waiting for the boss to show up again. She noted that Dom was missing, probably getting in trouble with the big boss again. That made her smile.

When the boss did show up, he looked over at everybody and nodded. "Now we can begin."

She wasn't sure what they would begin, but she looked over at Wallace to see him studying the boss curiously. Maybe Wallace didn't know what they were about to begin either. That concerned her a little more than she cared to admit. She waited, watching the boss curiously.

He walked over to Wallace and asked, "Remember what you said?"

"Which part?" he asked, with a note of humor.

"About finding others like you."

"Yeah, what about it?"

"I think I'll take some of your advice," he muttered. "I don't really want to be watching everybody twenty-four hours a day, and that seems to be what I'm heading for."

"It is exactly what you're heading for," Wallace declared, with a nod.

At that, Dominic walked in, the last bully to join the group. When he saw everybody sitting down and settled, almost in a friendly state, he snorted. "Who started the party and forgot to invite me?"

The boss shrugged. "Sometimes you're not welcome at the party."

Dominic glared at him. "Just remember that I *am* the party."

"You are, until we find somebody to replace you."

At that, Dominic glared at his boss. "You're talking

about replacing me?" he asked. Such a note of incredulity filled his tone that it was obvious such a travesty had never occurred to him. He turned and pointed a finger at Wallace. "Is this your doing?"

Wallace stared at him. "What have I got to do with any of this?" he asked, motioning around the room. "This is your game, not mine."

"Yeah, you better believe it," Dom declared, with a sneer. He then turned to the boss. "Forget it. You're not replacing me."

"I'll decide," the boss replied mildly, but his gaze was watchful.

Suddenly an odd thickening of the air filled the room.

Amy had heard that idiom used before and had never really understood what it meant, but now she did. She actually felt emotions were alive and well in this room. She felt *feelings*, as if tangible objects. Wow. She actually sensed this humanlike change in the atmosphere itself. She wondered if Terk had caused this shift. At that thought, she frowned. She hoped it was a good change, but she feared it was something ominous. She shifted ever-so-slightly closer to Wallace, wondering what the hell had just happened.

It was akin to watching men rattle sabers or something similar; another phrase she had heard and hadn't ever seen or thought about much before, but now understood exactly what that meant too. She watched as Dominic and the boss man stared at each other, and then the boss laughed.

"Whatever," he said, with a wave of his hand to Dom. "You can stay as long as you cooperate."

Amy frowned. She wanted to glance at Terk and Wallace without anyone noticing but decided against it right now. Had Dom changed the atmosphere in the room with his anger, his fear? She would have to ask Wallace and Terk about that later. Then she backtracked, trying hard not to shake her head for all to see. No way in hell was Dom this good at energy work. No, this had Terk's name written all over it. And, if the boss man thought Dom was doing this, all the better. Could be just woo-woo enough to give the boss man even more reasons to not trust Dom.

"Since when have I not cooperated?" Dominic asked, his gaze narrowing at the boss man.

"Damn near every day," the boss stated, with a long-suffering sigh. "Constantly bothering me with petty issues that really aren't worth my time."

"Like what?" Dom asked in astonishment.

She wasn't sure what had just happened. She couldn't help but glance from Terk to Wallace, and that glance gave her insight that they were doing something on an energy level, probably nonstop. She knew by that weird expression of concentration on both their faces, yet almost a blandness to their gazes. Not wanting to draw any attention to them, she made sure to avoid looking directly at them but studied the kidnappers in front of her instead. If Terk and Wallace were doing something, would it blow up in their faces or would it get them out of here?

She knew that they were obviously attempting to do something that would free them, but that didn't mean it would be quite as successful as they hoped. Dealing with bad men like this didn't ever turn out exactly the way they wanted it to. These power-hungry, money-hungry assholes always waited for the next opportunity to take charge and to be in control.

Amy watched for the ensuing fireworks, and they weren't long in coming.

The boss looked around at everybody and announced, "Here's the deal. Nothing's to change for the next couple days," he murmured. "I want them kept here, kept quiet, and you better feed and look after them. Do not injure any of them," he added, with a note of warning.

The men looked at each other, frowned, then over at Dominic, who was barely holding back the sneer from his face.

She wondered what the hell was going on, but some power play was happening here that she didn't quite understand.

The boss walked over to Dominic, speaking directly to him. "You especially. Leave them alone."

"What's this? They're your pets now?" Dominic asked in a taunting voice. "You trust them over me? Even though I've been working with you all this time, suddenly you don't trust me?"

"I didn't say I don't trust you," he clarified. "I'm just telling you, very specifically, to leave them alone. Whether I trust you or not, I do know what you can be like, and I don't want them hurt." And, with that, the boss man turned and strode out again.

Dominic turned to them. "What the hell did you do to him?"

Wallace stared at him. "What do you think we did? Nothing, of course."

Dominic snorted. "I'm not as gullible as he is. I don't quite understand what you might have been able to do, but I do know that some people can do all kinds of shit, and right now it seems to me as if you're trying to shuffle the deck."

"Even if we were," Wallace suggested, with unexpected humor, "what would you expect us to do? We are your prisoners, after all."

Dom nodded. "Yeah, but I don't think the boss thought of that. He doesn't really understand just what can be done in this world."

"And you do?" Terk asked curiously.

Dom again nodded, a smirk on his face. "I do. I've certainly seen a lot of psychics and what they can do, and I've certainly heard about even more," he declared in a controlled fury. "Some crazy dude worked for the US government who could do all kinds of shit. He would be awesome to work with, but you could never trust him."

"Why is that?" Terk asked, his voice lowering softly.

At that point, she realized it must be Terk himself who Dom was talking about.

Dominic sneered. "Think about it. Do you want to work for somebody you can't trust?"

"Why couldn't you trust him?" Wallace asked in the same confused tone. "This guy, what did he ever do to you?"

"He didn't do anything, but I wouldn't let him do anything either. You couldn't trust somebody like that, couldn't let him into your inner circle, because you don't know what he can do. If you don't know what people can do, they're dangerous."

"Ah, well, that is a good point," Terk agreed, with a nod of his head. "Such an interesting concept."

"Not a concept at all," Dom argued, with a sneer. "It's a simple fact."

"So, can we go back to our rooms now or have a cup of coffee at least?" Amy asked the guards, who were standing around, looking as if they were wondering what they were supposed to do next.

"You don't need coffee," Dominic declared.

"And yet that would hardly be considered *looking after us*, now would it?" she asked, with a wry tone. "So, who'll be the first one the boss man fires—or shoots—when I tell him that we couldn't even get a cup of coffee because Dom said so?" At that, Dominic strode to her, glaring down on her, trying to intimidate her possibly. She shrugged. "You think you can scare me by standing over me?" She shook her head. "I heard what the boss man said myself, as did you guys."

Dom snarled at her. "Sure, you may have heard all kinds of things, but that doesn't mean anybody listens to him. You think we don't know what he's like? You think we don't watch him to see where his weaknesses are?"

She stared at him. "Oh my, you're trying to cut him out, aren't you?"

He stiffened and glared at her. "Did you just read my mind?"

She snorted. "I don't need to be psychic for that. You're the scheming type, trying to figure out how to cut him out and then take over his contacts. It's a thought, but probably not a smart idea."

"Why is that?" he asked curiously.

"The boss man managed to get into that position somehow, even without psychic abilities. His forte seems to be money and brute force. So I presume the boss man has a bunch of rich backers, funding all this. Do you have that, Dom?" When he failed to answer her, she chuckled. "He obviously has something you don't, Dom. So he probably understands exactly what guys like you are up to."

Dom glared at her. "You don't know anything about me, and you don't know what guys like me are thinking," he snapped, followed by that same sneer again.

"No, probably not," she conceded, "and I'll take that as

a good thing."

He shook his head. "Why don't you just shut the fuck up?" She glared at him, and he laughed. "And that upsets you? You get upset to finally be told off after you've been talking nonstop this whole time? Wow," he muttered, as he looked over at Wallace. "Why, man? Why her?"

Wallace laughed. "Why not her? She's pretty special."

"Sure, but pretty *crazy* is more like it." Dom shook his head, turning to Amy now. "I don't even know why he would want to keep you around."

"Because you don't think like Wallace," she explained in a bored tone, hopping to her feet.

Dom stepped back suddenly at her quick movement.

This time she laughed at the absurdity of the situation. "What's the matter now? I'm five four and weigh 110 pounds. Really someone to fear, right?"

"I wasn't scared," Dom stated defiantly. "You startled me."

"Startling you is one thing," she replied, "but having that coffee right over there and not being allowed a cup? Well, that's just pissing me off." She walked over to the coffee, where the guards stood, and defiantly poured three cups, emptying the pot. Nobody made a move to stop her. She carried the first cup to Terk. Then she picked up the last two cups, handing one to Wallace. Nobody said anything, but she felt a brewing sense of opposition to her actions. She smiled at the men, then chuckled. "Thanks for the coffee." She injected just enough sincerity that it would not only confuse them but also make it harder for them to rise up against her.

She sat back down next to Wallace, who reached out an arm and tucked her up close. Snuggled up against his chest and holding the coffee cup in her hand, she wondered at the sense of self-satisfaction she felt, if that was even the correct wording.

She glanced around the room, sensing a touch of that weirdness again. Then she smiled, realizing that Terk and Wallace were manipulating the energy, manipulating the tone, the atmosphere, just to freak out Dom and their guards. If it would help them out of here, she was all for it.

Dominic just glared at her. "That was a pretty ballsy thing to do."

"Getting coffee?" She snorted, then shook her head. "I wanted a cup of coffee. The boss didn't say we couldn't have it, so it was hardly an issue."

"Not an issue as far as you're concerned, no," Dom conceded, "but as far as the guys who made the coffee, that's a different story."

"Why is that?" she asked, looking over at them. "Don't they share?"

"Not everybody shares," Dom snapped. "Some of these guys are not accustomed to sharing at all."

She didn't say anything, just shrugged. What was she supposed to say, since it was obvious that something was going on here?

Dominic turned to the others. "I'll take off for a bit. You know your orders."

"Yeah, we know our orders," one of the men replied, studying him. "But what we don't know is where you fit into all this. Is she right? Are you trying to take over?"

"If I was, what would it mean to you?" Dom asked, eyeing the men with curiosity.

He shrugged. "We just want to know where we'll end up at the end of the day." He motioned at his buddies and himself. "The last thing we want is to get caught in a power struggle—or an exchange of fire that doesn't have anything to do with us."

"Ah, so you want to know if you'll survive the end of this?" Dom stated. "Sure, you will, if you took care of the guy in the hospital, that is."

The other man shrugged. "He's under guard right now, so we have to wait a bit for an opportunity."

"Confirm that you do," Dom snapped. "No matter who ends up where at the end of the day, none of us will be happy if that guy gets loose." And, with that, Dom stormed out, one of the guards following him.

She looked over at the two remaining guards. "That doesn't make it easy on you, does it?" she asked. "Two bosses, not happy with the other, fighting. You wonder who'll be standing at the end of this. Plus, will Dom pay you what the boss man is paying you?"

One of them frowned at her.

She nodded. "I know. I get it. It's none of my business. But, at the end of the day, you have to ask yourself these questions."

"Doesn't matter if we ask ourselves or not," interjected the second man, who hadn't spoken up before. Even now his tone was wary as he added, "It's not as if we just get to walk away."

"Right," she agreed, again sensing the atmosphere shifting, giving the room a haunted vibe. It was pretty impressive. Changing from genial to almost empathetic now, she pressed on. "I'm sure this infighting was not what you signed on for."

Both men looked at each other, then over at her and nodded. "The boss, he's been fine," the first guard said, "but he got weird when it came to this."

"He had a vision in his mind, I think," she suggested. "So walking away from something he was pretty sure he could have makes it difficult."

The guard shook his head. "And yet what the hell does he want from all this? Who wants to deal with psychics who can read your mind? Who wants to deal with people who can do all kinds of crazy unbelievable shit—or anything else we've been hearing about?" He visibly shuddered. "I would just as soon know that the people in my world can't play those games."

"That's because you're a straight shooter," she noted, "but your bosses aren't. They want things bigger, better, and bolder. And that's where the problem comes in."

"It doesn't matter much," the other guard added, pouring himself some freshly made coffee. "We've got to deal with what we've got right now."

"Protect yourselves," she murmured. "Whenever those two go against each other, and things blow up, whoever remains will determine where you two stand, right?"

They nodded. "We get it," the one guard replied, "but you're in the same situation. So you should be worrying about yourself."

"Yeah, wouldn't that be nice," she muttered, with a laugh. "Sometimes we just don't get those options, do we?"

"Are you psychic too?" he asked. "It didn't seem like you were, when you were here last time."

She shook her head. "Nope, not me. I did see the guy you guys put in the hospital though. That sucked."

"That was the boss, the big boss," the other guard declared absentmindedly, as he sipped his coffee. "He's pretty-damn scary when he wants to be."

That tidbit was odd. "That surprises me," she shared. "I guess I figured he would have had one of you guys do that job."

The one guard shook his head. "Nope, not his style. When it comes to handing out the punishment, he likes to get his hands dirty," he shared, with an eye roll. "A little too dirty."

"Did you ever think about what the world would be like if he did get ahold of psychics he could use and abuse?" she asked curiously.

They nodded. "Yeah, but you also must understand what he's like regardless and choose which side will favor our world. It's not as if we can just turn around and walk out, even if you think you'll try to persuade us to do that," he pointed out bitterly. "It's not happening. It can't happen. The penalty for that would be incredibly harsh."

"Of course," she agreed sympathetically. She did feel bad for them—not bad enough though, not after what they'd done to her. But she understood that they were caught between a rock and a hard place as well. "There's really no easy answer when you're stuck in the middle, is there?"

"Nope, there sure isn't." He tossed back the rest of his coffee, then looked over at her. "A word of advice. You really need to keep your mouth quiet when he's around because he has a very short temper. When it blows, everybody and everything around him ducks. You could be caught in that crossfire and not see tomorrow—literally. And believe me that the boss man wouldn't give a crap. Not one bit." And, with that warning, he looked over at his buddy and added, "We need to get them back to their rooms."

His buddy nodded, looked over at their captives, and realized that there was three of them to only the two guards.

He frowned and asked, "Where'd Tom go?"

"He went out with the boss. You want to go get him?"

"Yeah, but …"

"I'll go." The one guard walked over to the door. "You keep an eye on them." And, with that, he quickly dashed out.

Now just the one guard was left, and he stared around at the three prisoners. "Did he do that on purpose?" he asked, studying them carefully.

"Probably," Wallace agreed, as he stood up and stretched.

The guard shifted back uneasily. "Well, crap."

"They didn't think that through very well, did they?" Wallace asked, as he took a step toward him.

"They'll be back any second anyway," the guard stated, showing a bit of bravado. "Besides, I'm sure I can take you."

"Of course, but can you take all three of us?"

"She's a piece of cake, hardly even worth bringing into the picture. But the two of you? Yeah, I've done that before. Even making me go through the motions will piss me off, and you'll pay for it."

"Ah," she muttered, "there we go, threats and more threats. Same old, same old again. Every time I turn around, somebody is threatening somebody," she muttered. Then she turned to study Wallace for a moment. "What are the chances that we are being watched?"

"Probably pretty good," he said, as he flexed his fists.

The second guard suddenly reappeared, glaring at everybody. "Wow, what's this? You had an opportunity to have a dustup, and you didn't even try it?" he asked, with a laugh.

Wallace shrugged. "No challenge with just one," he muttered. "But now that you're back—" Without warning, he swung his right fist and took out the second guard, with a hard crack to his jaw.

He crashed to the floor without even making a sound.

The first guard stared at him in shock.

Wallace gave him an evil grin. "You're next."

And, with that, the guard bolted for the doorway.

WALLACE LAUGHED AS he grabbed the retreating guard, gripping him like a cat by the scruff of the neck as he pulled him back and gave him a fist to his face too. He dropped him to the floor and in a moment sent him packing, the same as his buddy. He looked over at Terk. "That was easy."

Terk nodded. "Once you shift the energy, plant those seeds of doubt," he murmured, "they don't have much in the way of defenses against it."

"I could feel it," Amy exclaimed, staring at him. "I just didn't know what you were doing."

"Yet you were working in sync with us. Wallace and I were giving them a chance to rethink their life choices," Terk shared, with a wry look in her direction. "I'm not a pacifist by any means, but it's definitely the only way out of some situations."

Wallace turned and looked at the doorway. He glanced over at Terk. "You have any reading on where the boss is right now?"

"He's waiting," Terk replied. "This was the test."

"Yet he doesn't even know what he's testing, does he?"

"No, but he's hoping for something conclusive, maybe something that will give him an idea if this is worth pursuing, if we have any abilities that can help him."

"Yet this wasn't that much of a test," Amy noted, staring at him. "Not that I want to denigrate what Wallace has just done, but … surely a lot of guys could have done this without too much trouble."

Wallace snorted and gave her an amused glance.

She raised her arms in frustration. "I'm not trying to insult you, but it's not as if this took energy work."

"Not the physical fight, it didn't," Terk agreed, with a smile. "Even if any energy work was used, it's not something they would recognize."

"Right," she noted, "and I didn't get an impression that this place was wired to interfere with that."

"It was," Wallace pointed out cheerfully. "We took that out first. So no eyes or ears on this room."

She grinned. "Always nice to work with pros."

"Yep." Wallace laughed. "That's one of the first rules."

"Sounds good," she muttered, and then she laughed in amusement. "When you think about it, there's an awful lot of things still to learn, isn't there?"

At that, Terk nodded. "The day we stop learning, we'll be dead. The field we're in? … It always changes, day in and day out, absolutely no break. Just understand that there's no stopping this craziness either. It continues to grow constantly as well."

"Maybe that's okay too," she murmured, then she stepped forward. "Why don't I go out first?"

"What good will that do?" Wallace exclaimed, glaring at her. "That'll just put you in danger."

She laughed. "They won't hurt me, remember? I'm just the bait to keep you cooperative." And, with that, she smiled at the two of them. "Back in a sec." She opened the door, and leaving it open, stepped out into the hallway.

Wallace went to follow her, but Terk grabbed him and murmured, "You might not like it, but she's right. They won't take her out or hurt her badly, at least not right now."

"Hurt her badly?" Wallace repeated. "Did you hear yourself?"

"Yep, sure did," Terk replied. "I'm not sensing any danger around her at the moment though."

Wallace shifted, checked in with his own senses, then nodded. "Agreed. … Interesting work you got here," he quipped, with a glance back at Terk.

"Yeah, you want more of it?" Terk asked. "I could use somebody who knows how to knock out assholes in a one-two punch."

"You mean two for two?"

"Yeah, two for two works. The faster, the easier, and the less stressful it is for everybody."

"Yet we don't even know where Jonas currently is."

"I'm going there first," Terk stated, with a casual look around. "As much as we might have our issues at times, I would never leave him behind."

"Good," Wallace said, "because I sure wouldn't do any work for you if I thought you would."

He laughed. "We're an odd pair left in this world. … Not a whole lot of honor among thieves anymore."

"Good thing we're not thieves," Wallace pointed out.

Just then, Amy popped her head back in and grinned at them. "All clear."

Terk sighed. "That's bad news."

The smile fell from her face. "Okay, you need to explain that then," she snapped, a bit abashed. "I was feeling pretty darn cheeky that nobody was out here waiting for us."

"So where are they then?" Terk asked.

She frowned and muttered, "Oh shit, ... *Jonas.*"

"Yeah, ... Jonas."

They stepped out into the hallway, and Terk motioned to the left. She looked over at him and shook her head. "I don't think so." He raised an eyebrow, and she murmured, "I hear a weird hum going on."

"I noticed it," Terk replied, "but what are you saying?"

"I think they're using us to track to him, hoping we can find him, which will allow them to know if we know something or not."

"And?" he asked patiently, his gaze intense.

She took a deep breath, and Wallace had to admire that she was even bucking Terk. It's not that you couldn't talk to Terk, but, in a situation like this, she seemed to be almost questioning his judgment.

"I think they're trying to send you in one direction, or at least confuse your signals in one or even more ways."

"Yes, they are being confused," Terk confirmed. "I did compensate for that, but tell me where you think we should go."

She hesitated and pointed in the opposite direction.

"Why?" he asked curiously. Again she hesitated. "Tell me, and not just that. ... Give me a solid reason, and I'm happy to try it."

She gave him a quick grin. "Because I can feel him."

His gaze narrowed. "You can feel who?"

"I can feel Jonas," she stated in a low tone.

"Good enough." Terk nodded. "Let's go."

With that, he made an about-turn and headed in the direction she had suggested. Wallace, his eyebrows shooting up, looked at her in surprise. She shrugged. "I don't always get any answers," she murmured, "but, when I do, they're quite strong."

"Good, and I like the conviction that went with it." Wallace sent her a smile.

She laughed as they walked forward. "I don't know about conviction," she clarified, "but there's a sense of timing right now. There's an urgency involved."

"No doubt." Wallace groaned. "When isn't there with people like this?"

She nodded. "Jonas is okay, but I don't know that they'll keep him that way."

"They don't plan to, but two guards are down, courtesy of Wallace, so we can count on at least two guards up ahead. So Dom and the boss man are around somewhere nearby."

She thought about it and agreed. "That's all I'm getting for numbers too."

Terk nodded. "So, that makes three of us against potentially all three of them."

"Good," she murmured. "Glad to know we're at least in agreement on that much."

As they headed down the hallway, Wallace watched as she hesitated. He grabbed her hand. "When you have a conviction, you stick to it," he stated. "We can always change direction but only if you feel it."

"What if we're heading into a trap?" she asked, with a wry look in his direction.

"Then we're heading into a trap, but we have to try this anyway, so remember that. Most importantly, we already know it."

She didn't say anything.

Wallace asked, "That accident you had, what did it do to you?"

"You mean, what didn't it do?" she muttered. "Seems as

if it ripped off a huge Band-Aid, exposing a fresh wound."

Terk looked over at her and grinned. "That's a really good analogy because that's how we often felt when we were healing after being attacked. Everything felt wide open, raw even."

"Exactly," she agreed, with a shudder. "There's … this sense of not being able to shut anything down, not being able to control everything that's flying at you." With a sigh, she continued on.

They walked a good twenty yards, and she stopped again. Terk raised an eyebrow.

She frowned. "He's being moved."

"Ah, that would explain it."

"Explain what?"

"I feel energy shifting. Two bodies, but I don't know how many we were dealing with right now."

"I'm not even sure I'm getting two bodies out of this," she admitted. "But definitely a feeling of … somebody being moved somewhere."

"They're trying to keep Jonas on the move to see if we can track him," Terk suggested.

"That's a shitty thing to do," she murmured, and then she laughed. "But that's all they really want to know, isn't it?"

"Yeah, and that's also what we don't want to reveal," Wallace pitched in.

Terk nodded at that. "So, if we continue in this direction, we'll have to find a way to save Jonas, then afterward not reveal anything."

"You mean, from them having a good idea of what we can do?" she muttered. "So, how will you do that? You don't have a mind-wipe handy, do you?"

He grinned. "No, and it's not exactly ethical either."

"No, maybe not," she muttered. "Still, I sure wouldn't mind getting rid of some of these people who seem to think playing games with lives is okay."

As they came up to two doors, she motioned to the left, only to realize Terk's hand was already reaching for it. Wallace watched in amusement as the two balanced each other out in this dance. Wallace was also getting the same vibes as the two of them but didn't feel the need to get in the middle of it. Yet it was nice to have his skills validated by these two.

Wallace wondered if Terk was testing her too. That would make sense, and, considering everything she had been through, there had to be some question as to where her state of mind was at, as well as her energy-worker skills. Like Terk, Wallace had a lot of questions about Amy's accident, about her more recent illness, and what she ended up with as gifts afterward.

Almost as if she knew his thoughts, she looked over at Wallace and smiled brightly. "I know. We need to have a talk."

He gave a soft laugh. "I would love to talk," he replied, then sobered. "I definitely want to ask you about a lot of things."

"It's not really an issue we need to deal with right now though," she murmured, as she looked at the door slowly opening in front of them. "Are you ready for company?"

"Always."

And rather than just going in, they waited. Terk looked over at Wallace, with a note of amusement.

"Right, I'm the muscle," Wallace muttered with an eyeroll, as he stepped forward into the room. There he found

Jonas and one of the two other guards.

The guard looked at him in triumph and smiled. "Well, well, what a lovely surprise."

"And yet it's not a surprise to see you," Wallace stated. "After all, how many others can be left behind? You're the one who walked away with the boss. You're the one who didn't stick around to see if the other two guards would end up in a fight with us."

"Of course not. Why would I do that?" He laughed. "It's obvious that you knew what you were doing, and even the best street fighter, unless he's professional, won't do well up against a lot of military training," he pointed out. "I certainly don't have that training. What I do have, however, is this." With that, he brandished a weapon.

She looked at it as she came up behind Wallace and stared. "Oh, so somebody finally brought a gun to this fight, *huh*?" She shook her head. "You guys really suck, don't you?"

He stared at her. "That's enough out of you," he snapped, getting angry.

She shrugged. "I don't think so. I just think you guys are a piece of shit for all the chaos you've been causing. All you are really doing is trying to figure out whether you can catch any us doing anything."

"Dominic said you couldn't," he shared, with a sneer.

"Oh good." She gave him a big grin. "That's nice to know."

"What do you mean, it's nice to know?" he asked, eyeing her warily.

"*This*," she declared. Then she stepped forward and placed a hand on Wallace, who then placed a hand on Terk.

The guard frowned at them and asked, "What is this? What are you three doing?"

Terk reached out his hand, and a beam of something hit the gunman.

The armed guard tried to react, taking a step forward, then slowly fell to his knees and went down. "But …" His eyes rolled into the back of his head, and he collapsed.

She smiled at the man down on the floor. "Glad you got the message."

"Haven't done that trick in a long time," Terk shared, with amusement. "And," he added, gazing at her sharply, "that was a pretty strong energy bolt you sent."

"I didn't know whether it lost force when transferred from me to you to you—or slowed down with each transfer to each person—so I amped it up to begin with." She shrugged, frowning at Terk. "But you got the energy right away."

"I tend to," he said, "so just keep that in mind."

"Good, it makes life easier."

"It does, indeed." Terk walked over, kicked away the gunman's weapon, then bent down to check on him.

While Terk was squatted next to the guard, Amy looked up to the open doorway behind them, now filled with the boss and Dominic.

"See? I told you," Dominic exclaimed. "They both have abilities."

Dom had such a smug look on his face that she wanted to plow one into him.

"She doesn't, of course," Dom stated, with a dismissive wave of his hand. "But these two? Now that's interesting."

The boss looked at his captives and then at his man on the ground. "Did you really just do that?"

"Do what?" Terk asked, as he checked over the guy on the ground. "What are you feeding these guys? It looks as if he had a heart attack or something. Did you see the way his eyes rolled up?" Terk pointed out, with a casual shrug. "That definitely doesn't seem normal." He frowned. "You better get some medical help for him, you know, if you need him."

"Medical help?" Dominic asked, with a searing look. "Like hell. You did that."

"I didn't do anything," Terk replied, staring at him in astonishment. "What the hell do you think we are?"

Dominic shook his head. "No, no, no, no, no. You don't get to do that."

"Don't get to do what?" Terk asked, standing up and giving Dominic an innocent expression, with some astonishment added in for good measure.

Wallace wanted to laugh. It was obvious that their kidnappers were hoping to get answers and thought to get somebody to admit something. It was just as obvious that nobody here would have anything to say.

Terk looked around the room. "If you don't get help for him, … he may not survive."

"That's fine," the boss replied. "You guys killed him so—"

"Actually we didn't," Terk corrected, frowning at him. "We didn't have anything to do with this." He looked over to Jonas, sitting on the floor, staring at everything in silence. "Jonas, did you see anything?"

Jonas shook his head and shrugged. "The guy just keeled over. Terk reached out a hand to stop him, but he hit the ground hard, before they even reached him."

Dominic started swearing. "Oh, no, no, no you don't," he yelled. "No way in hell."

"Don't you have it recorded somehow?" Terk asked.

The boss man faced Dom, who then nodded. "I do." He

pulled out his phone and brought up the security camera app. He walked closer to the boss and pointed at the screen. "See? Look. It'll be right here."

The four captives watched the two boss men, as the video was replayed. From his position, Wallace could barely see the movement of the figures on the screen. The gunman took half a step, an odd gait to it, and completely collapsed, just as Terk reached out a hand, as if to help.

At that, the boss looked over at Dominic and snorted. "Yeah? See what I see? The guy had a heart attack or something," he snapped, staring down at the guard. "I told him that he should lay off all that bloody fried food, but he didn't give a shit."

"No way, he was fine earlier. They did it," Dominic roared.

The boss shook his head and declared, "No, they didn't, and I'm done with this obsession of yours." The boss man sounded truly pissed. "If and when I find *real* psychics," he noted with emphasis, "I'll handle this in a whole different manner." Dominic glared at him, and the boss shook his head. "Enough. This nonsense is over with here and now. One more misstep, and you'll be dealing with cleaning up the rest of this mess on your own."

"Oh, yeah, and what will you do now?" Dom asked, with a sneer. "It's not as if you have any options. You've got MI6 kidnapped and all kinds of people here who will be testifying against you, if you leave them alive," he muttered.

The boss laughed. "Hey, I'm the one leaving the country, and chances of anyone finding me in my world are slim." He pointed at Dom. "You're the local. Why do you think I made sure that we played these games over here? As far as I'm concerned, you're the one who kidnapped everybody, and I'm just here at your mercy." The boss man took a step back. "I just escaped from an iffy deal gone bad here," he shared, "so I'm pretty sure I can also escape from any lies that you profess." He shook his head and laughed at Dom. And then he turned and disappeared so fast that they could barely react.

Dominic raced after him, calling out, but returned seconds later to find Wallace helping Jonas to the doorway. "Stop," Dominic cried out.

"Stop what?" Wallace asked in anger. "Haven't you figured out that the boss man's done with you? If you keep pursuing this, you'll end up getting a bullet, or maybe you just need that reality reinforced for you." He gave him an intense stare. "Go ahead. Go on after him. See how far you get."

Dominic stared at him and shook his head, glancing at the prone man on the floor. "What did you guys do?"

"What do you mean, what did we do?" Terk asked, staring at him. "I thought you were a psychic."

"But I don't know what you did," he cried out. "Or how you even did it."

"Maybe you don't need to know either," Amy added, staring at him. "You're nothing but a troublemaker, a liar, and a cheat. Believe me that *nobody* wants to work with you." She was calm and collected. "You've got three injured guards here, so you may want to take care of them. You wanted to get all this away from the boss man anyway, right? ... So here's your chance to pick up the pieces," she said, with a nonchalant shrug. "But remember this. If we find out about any more kidnappings of *psychics*, we'll know exactly who to look for."

Leaving him standing there, looking at them in shock,

they headed out the door. As they got down the hallway, she kept waiting for Dom to appear behind her. She asked Terk, "It can't really be that easy, can it?"

"I don't think so," Terk replied. "So, keep up your energy, while we get Jonas out of here," he murmured. "And let's find out where the boss man went."

"Ah, now that would make more sense."

They headed cautiously back down into the tunnels and went around several corners, finding Riff headed toward them.

He shook his head in exasperation. "Why do I even bother?"

At that, Terk laughed. "Because there's still an ambush coming our way," he added, with a wave of his hand. "You want to give me a hand with Jonas here?"

Riff asked him, "Jonas, what the hell?"

Jonas gave him a hard look. "A little assistance would be good."

But instead of just helping, Riff picked him up in his arms and turned around. "Come on. Let's get out of here," Riff stated. "I hate these creepy tunnels."

They hadn't gotten more than a few feet when somebody behind them called out.

Knowing it was the wrong thing to do but instinctively already in motion, Amy turned.

CHAPTER 10

AMY FOUND THE boss man looking at them in delight, a gun in his right hand, nonchalantly hanging at his side. Amy nodded. "I figured it was you. You've just been trying to get rid of Dominic."

"Dominic is small fry." He looked at her and the others. "Is this stuff for real?"

Terk replied cautiously, "It might be for real, but trying to wield it against somebody's free will simply won't work."

The boss man frowned at that and turned to Wallace. "You tried to tell me that earlier, didn't you?"

"Yeah, and you didn't listen."

He shrugged. "You told me to find a group who would work for me willingly."

"It's the only way it could ever work," Terk confirmed. "The more you try to coerce somebody, the less effective it will be."

He grouched at that. "I could still take you guys with me." He raised his gun to make that point.

"How do you expect that to happen?" Terk asked, with a cool bemusement.

"Why not? I have power. I have money, and I have the sheer might to make it happen. *I have a gun.*"

"In your right hand too. I see it, but there's more of us now," Amy pointed out, walking toward him. "What is it you think you'll do?"

"You just keep walking my way," the boss man declared, "and I'll show you."

"Don't do it," Wallace said to her, an urgent note of concern in his tone.

Amy nodded, smiling, but not taking her gaze off the boss man. "It's okay, Wallace."

Even Terk sent out a warning to her.

She nodded again, walking closer to the boss man. "See? They don't want me coming anywhere near you."

"That's because they know I'll just grab you and keep you close. Then they'll do anything I want," the boss declared, with a smirk.

"That's your faulty reasoning talking. You've discounted me completely, thinking I couldn't do anything because, in your mind, I'm just prey," she explained. "That's the thing with discounting someone this way. That prey can turn to predator very quickly, and, before you know it, it's too damn late." With that, she placed a hand on the side of his neck. "I get it. You don't know anything about this. You don't know anything about us. From your perspective this is all fun and games, but you don't see how serious it really is. You have no idea just how *very* serious this really is."

He laughed at that. "Good, in that case you can come with me and show me just how *serious it really is.*"

"No, no, and hell no. I don't want to go with you or with anybody like you. That isn't what I want to do with my life, so my answer is a resolute no."

He grabbed her by the arm. "I won't give you a choice."

She patted his cheek with her free hand and added, "I won't give you a choice either. Look at me."

He frowned down at her, gripping her arm even harder.

She snapped the fingers on her free hand, smiling all the while.

The resulting jolt made him jump.

She nodded. "See? You have these meridians that run up and down your system, and just a snap of my fingers sends the energy flowing in one direction or the other," she shared. "I can just as easily make the energy go the other way." With a snap of her fingers, he jolted again.

"What the hell?" he yelled, releasing his hold on her.

"This is what I warned you about. You thought you could hold me against my will, but really I'm holding you against yours." She patted his cheek again. "So, when you start playing games with people who have abilities, you might want to remember that they probably have more power than you do and can make you act like a puppet on a string. You may have the urge to ask why, and I will say this one time only, so hear me well. *Because they can*," she declared, as she snapped her fingers yet again. "And so can I."

He jolted once more and took a step back from her.

She nodded. "Now I've got your energy pattern. I have a lock on it, so guess what? You can run, but you can't hide. You can get to the end of this hallway, and I can snap my fingers and make you dance and do things you don't want to do. So, if I ever see you again on this side of the ocean—or anywhere in the world, for that matter—just remember. All I need to do is snap my fingers."

She did it again.

He jolted again, the corner of his lips floundering, as if he were having a stroke.

She nodded. "When you play with energy, there are often repercussions, which can do much damage, can cause a stroke even. How would you feel about losing all control of your left side?" she asked, staring at him intently. "Are you okay with never speaking normally again?"

"Whoa, whoa, whoa," he mumbled, as he stepped back once more. "That's ... that's not possible."

"What? That you can have a stroke? You're having a stroke right now," she stated, "and that's a whole different story. You see? A stroke is caused by a blockage of your heart, so just a snap of my fingers—not everybody's fingers but my fingers—can make you have a stroke, like you are experiencing right now."

She stared straight at the boss man. "And you know something? I'm okay with that because I'm a little tired of you guys pushing me around, trying to do things with my friends and using me to hurt people. I'm fed up with you, trying to use me to get what you want. So, ... until we come to an understanding, I'll just keep doing this." That warning given, she snapped her fingers.

His body jolted even harder, his face now flushed and his left arm twitching. He cried out in pain.

"So, are you in agreement?" she asked.

He struggled to answer verbally, but instead he nodded frantically.

"I'm sorry," she said. "That doesn't do it for me. I need more of an answer than that."

"I ... *weave* ... you *awone*," he mumbled.

"I didn't quite hear you," she called out.

"I ... *weave* ... you *awone*," he cried out louder this time, stepping back to get farther away from her, almost frantic to get out of her sight.

"Oh, one more thing, just in case you think this is a *reach* thing," she added, snapping her fingers one more time.

Even though he'd backed up a good ten feet, he still danced in place. "It's not about distance. That gun of yours? It's all about energy, and that weapon won't work anymore." She pointed at it. "Go ahead and fire it. I really don't give a shit."

He frowned at her, looked down at his gun, and lifted it, as if forgetting that he even had it. He fired at her, once, twice, three times, but it did nothing. It just made a weird clicking sound. He stared at it, stared at her, made an odd sound, then turned and tried to run. However, his body was dealing with the recent stroke effects, hitting him even now, and he slowly crumbled to the ground about twenty feet away.

She turned to the other men, her temper still evident. "Yes, he's having a real stroke." She sounded calm, but her aura was barking mad. "So, it's up to you guys whether we get him medical help or we just leave him to die in the tunnels, like he left poor Gerry," she muttered.

Riff looked at her with a newfound respect. "I know what I vote for, but it's really not up to me." He looked down at Jonas, held in his arm, and asked, "What do you want to do?"

He looked over at her. "I'll get a team in here right away. We don't want assholes like this running around." He turned to Riff and tapped his pocket. "I'll need a phone." Riff helped pull out Jonas's phone searching for a signal. There was a single bar but it was enough. Very quickly he had a team on their way.

She looked around at the others. "Just in case any of you feel like judging me for that ..."

Immediately Terk shook his head. "I'm not judging you. I don't think any of us are." He added, "Cool trick, by the way."

"It is," she agreed, with a smile, "though it's not one I tend to use often."

"Yeah, I'm not surprised," Terk muttered. "How far is the range of your effectiveness?"

She looked at him and then sighed. "I haven't tested it, to be honest, but I'm pretty sure there's no limit." Terk stared at her in fascination, and she nodded. "So, the next time you get pissed at me ..."

Terk burst out laughing. "Yeah, we all have skills and techniques that can create all kinds of hell on earth. I'm not afraid of you any more than you're afraid of me because we all have kept our humanity."

She grinned. "It would be awfully nice to know that people out there aren't afraid of me."

"For that, you really need to join my team."

Jonas grumbled, turned to glare at Terk, then asked Amy, "Hey, what about my team?"

"Oh, you mean the team you already turned me down for?" she asked, frowning at him.

"I didn't know you could do all that," he replied. "Why didn't you just tell me?"

"Are you serious?" she asked, her eyebrows raised. "Why would I tell you? That just sounds like a bad deal for me."

He rolled his eyes at that, and Terk laughed.

"Jonas, you need to give it up. Anybody in this field needs me, not you."

Jonas shook his head. "The powers that be, they were thinking that *both* could work out. You know that you could have your team, and we could have ours."

"Yeah, but it'll take somebody like me to lead it."

At that, Jonas eyed him hopefully. "As it turns out, I wanted to ask you about that."

"About what?" Terk asked warily.

Jonas shook his head. "Would you run our team for us? Official government status and all that other good stuff."

At that, Riff snorted. "If he does, he'll lose half his men," he declared.

Jonas glared at him. "Nobody's asking you."

"You may not be asking me, but we've already been there, working for the government. As you may recall, it ended badly," Riff reminded him, "so the answer is no. Why is it, whenever you guys get anything, you try to control it? As you should see from what just happened here, controlling us doesn't work so well."

Jonas winced and nodded. "Still, that doesn't mean I'm done talking about it," he called out, as Terk continued to walk toward the end of the tunnel.

"You better be done talking about it," Riff stated. "Otherwise I'm not helping you out of here. I'll leave you right here on the sewer floor."

Jonas groaned. "You guys are all mad."

"Maybe, but we're *good* mad, so remember that."

And, with that, Riff carried Jonas toward the light.

"DID YOU MEAN it?" Amy asked Terk. "About coming to work for you?"

He nodded. "Yep, I sure did. We've got a lot of people working and living together, so getting along is the order of the day."

"I can understand that," she replied, "and my gifts are still rusty in many ways."

He laughed. "Not in any of the ways that I saw," he

murmured. "I've never seen that trick before."

She snorted. "It's pretty easy. Once I realized what it could do, I knew just how much of a problem it was for other people."

"Of course," Terk agreed. "It's one thing to have that control, but it's another thing completely to let people know you can do that."

"And know that he's had a *stroke*," she added, making air quotes, "but I don't know if he's safe to have that knowledge."

"After they treat him, we can see what shape he's in," he murmured. "However, don't ever feel bad about self-defense. You have the right to live your life as you choose, and it's not fair if other people keep trying to take that freedom away from you."

"It may not be fair," she murmured, "but you and I both know it happens constantly."

"But we don't have to let them get away with it," Terk stated. "That's partly why we do what we do."

"I do love that," she said, with a smile. "It's definitely heartwarming to know that people like me are living a more normal life than I ever thought possible."

"I'm glad to hear that too," Terk noted. "There's plenty of room for all of us in this world, and you've just got to let people know that you won't be pushed around. I think you did that effectively today."

She laughed. "It felt good in a way. I'd forgotten what it was like to utilize that energy."

"Have you ever had to do that before?"

She shook her head. "No, I haven't had to, though that doesn't mean I didn't want to a time or two," she muttered. "I suppose Jonas will be on my case constantly because I didn't tell him that I could do that."

Wallace walked closer and reached out an arm. She looked up, smiled, and hooked hers through his. He squeezed her hand. "Of course you didn't. That's the kind of thing we keep under wraps. We're more open between us and Terk and his team as relationships and as trust develops, but as far as the rest of the world is concerned? Not only no, but hell no."

She nodded. "That was part of my problem with being isolated so much when my gifts changed. That was a big one."

"In what way did your gifts change though?" Terk asked. "I thought you could always do this and the rest."

"Yeah, but now I can do it without trying," she muttered. "It's almost too easy, as in, I have to control my temper and never get to that point."

"That goes for all of us," Terk noted. "We all have abilities that require control, and that's one of the reasons I have the place that I do, because then we have a safe home base, where people can learn that kind of control. Otherwise power without control is just abusive, and that's not what we want at all. That's not who we are."

"Got it." She chuckled. "I agree wholeheartedly."

"Good," he replied. "So, in that case, can I tell them at home that the apartment should become permanent then?"

She stared at him. "Is that an option?"

"It is as far as I'm concerned, so you tell me."

She smiled. "I would love for it to become an option," she clarified, smiling, as she looked back at Wallace. "What about you?"

He laughed. "You tell me. As far as the group is concerned, we're already an item."

She winced. "I did get that impression."

"How could you not? We got the suite with adjoining rooms after all."

"But I wasn't sure if you were okay with that."

He gave her a quick grin. "Honey, if I wasn't okay with it, I would have changed it on the first night."

"Good," she said, "because it's definitely how I want it."

"Perfect." He leaned over and gave her a big kiss. "Now"—Wallace turned to Terk—"do you think we could possibly get the hell out of here? We could use a couple days away, just to figure out our life, you know?"

"Or you could just spend a few days at the castle, settling in," Terk replied. "That's almost a holiday in itself."

Jonas burst out laughing. "Like hell," he muttered, his laughter now a coughing fit. "So much chaos is going on in that castle at any given time, I can't imagine you'll want to spend all your time there."

"Maybe not," Amy conceded, "but it would be nice to have a home base and to know that it really is home."

"Exactly," Wallace agreed, "so it's all good. Let's get the hell out of here and go home then."

And that's exactly what they did.

CHAPTER 11

A MY HEADED FOR the shower, as soon as she arrived at the castle, as did Wallace, Terk, and Riff. That smell had to go. When Amy finally walked into her bedroom that night, she sat down on the bed, wondering at the quick change in her circumstances. She did feel safe here. She did feel a part of something bigger than herself, and yet it was something that she didn't quite understand.

Such a team feeling encased this whole castle that she found herself a little hesitant, wondering if maybe she didn't quite have what it took. She also knew that everybody else would slam her for even thinking that, and she didn't want to get caught up in that negative thinking, but it was hard not to when so much was going on all the time.

A lot of special people were here, and it would take her a while to even sort through their names because just so many lived here at the castle. There was also something weird going on with Riff, whom she'd only seen a couple times now, and this woman named Angela. She hung around Riff like a bad penny, and yet she seemed to be all heart and was here for the children constantly. Yet it seemed as if she was keeping a watchful eye on everything.

Nobody had really explained what was going on there, but Amy hoped that if she was here long enough, people would relax, and Amy would get a full, or at least partial, explanation, in time. As she contemplated all this, the door opened, and Wallace walked in. She smiled up at him. "Hey."

"How you doing?" he murmured, coming to sit beside her.

"I'm okay. It's been a crazy day though."

"Yeah, it has been," he agreed, with a laugh. "And that's okay. Crazy isn't so bad all the time." He reached out to hold her hand.

"Maybe not," she murmured, looking down at their joined hands, "but it's strange being here."

He nodded. "We can always go away for a few days if you want, or we can just stay here and acclimate."

"You know the acclimating part isn't a bad idea," she murmured. "We haven't had time to do that."

"No, we sure haven't," he agreed, with a laugh. "We haven't had time to do anything but say hello."

"What about Jonas?"

"As it turns out, I just came in to give you an update. He'll be fine. His broken leg has been set, and he's off duty for a while. He's already making noise about coming over here to get some healing done," he added, with an eye roll.

She stared at him and started to laugh. "That sounds like something I would do."

"Exactly." Wallace chuckled. "And why wouldn't you, knowing skilled healers are here?"

"Do you think Terk will have a problem with Jonas doing that?"

"No, not at all. Despite all the bantering and complaining back and forth, deep down I think he and Jonas are good friends. Another good thing is it looks like Gerry Wallace will pull through too. So good news all around."

She nodded. "That is great news. And I got that feeling myself about Terk and Jonas," she muttered. "I think Terk knows an awful lot of people."

"He does know an awful lot of people, but it's you I want to talk about tonight," he stated, with a smile, using his free hand to pat hers that he still held on to.

"And here I thought you were talking about Jonas," she said, with a teasing grin.

He chuckled. "I think we have a few things to discuss straightaway."

"What could that possibly be?" she quipped, narrowing her gaze at him. "Unless you'll piss me off immediately by telling me that we don't have anything between us or that you're unsure."

He stared at her, his jaw opening, but then it slowly closed.

She nodded. "Good, I didn't think you would be that foolish."

He stared at her for a moment. "What if I want reassurance?"

She blinked, but then she grinned. "You can have all the reassurance you need."

"Without snapping your fingers?" he asked.

She burst out laughing, only to become somber. "Are you scared of me?"

"Nope, definitely not," he replied comfortably, scooching closer to her. "I also have a few tricks up my own sleeve."

"Exactly. I figured you had all kinds of skills," she noted, with a laugh.

"But it's not skills that I was talking about," he clarified. "I was hoping for some, you know, *other* reassurance."

And he gave her such a pitiful look that she burst into a

fit of giggles, then straightened up, and, in a move that surprised both of them, shifted her position so she straddled him, sitting on his lap, her arms looped around his neck, and she smiled. "Reassurance, *huh*?" she repeated. "Are you telling me that you didn't see our energy entwine the whole time we were together?"

He nodded. "I did see it."

"Are you telling me that you didn't see our energy seeking each other out when we were apart?"

He nodded. "I did see that."

"Are you telling me that right now you can't see the energy between the two of us, blending and melding into something much better?" She leaned forward and nuzzled his nose with hers.

He grinned and said, "I do see that."

"Ooh, I do too," she agreed, then burst out laughing. She leaned over and kissed him. "Just in case you have any doubts, and you really do need that reassurance, we already have a relationship, and we can make it into whatever we want it to be. We have the power to make it something extra special because of who we are, what we can do, what we can see, what we feel, what we already know."

"*Huh.*"

"It's not as if we'll ever argue and give each other the cold shoulder—or not for long, not while living in this fish bowl of a castle full of psychics," she noted, chuckling. "It's not as if we'll drag out the tired old excuse of not knowing there's a problem, when we obviously will both know very well what's happening, good or bad. And living in this place? A ton of healing energy will be sent our way."

He wrapped his arms around her and pulled her tight up against his chest, dropping little kisses across her cheeks.

She smiled, feeling the warmth of his breath across her face, and snuggled in closer.

"That's true," he said, "and *positive* energy at that. We're on an amazing journey, and I can't imagine all that we have ahead of us."

She tilted her head and looked up at him. "We'll have everything we could ever want," she whispered.

He leaned over, kissed her deeply, his tongue warring gently with hers, and whispered, "So, about these adjoining rooms …"

"I'm surprised we're allowed to keep them," she muttered, looking around.

"I think they're planning to move us out of this suite into a big apartment—with one bedroom. In fact, they're getting one set up for us right now, providing we're okay with it."

She chuckled. "In that case"—she got up, pulling him to her bed—"we should christen this one. Then we'll move and christen that one as well."

He burst out laughing. "I really like the way you think."

Pushing him back onto the bed, she climbed on top of him, then sent him a gentle bolt of energy that moved down his back all the way to his toes. Moaning, he relaxed into the mattress. "Was that you?"

"It absolutely was," she whispered, as she leaned over and kissed him, licked the tip of his nose, and laughed, before stroking her hands up underneath his T-shirt. "You really are wearing too many clothes."

"Oh, I can take care of that in no time," he stated, as he shifted upright, even with her in his arms. He then sat her on the bed and quickly shucked off his clothing, but she was way faster. By the time he turned around, stark naked, she sat cross-legged on the bed, already fully nude. He shook his head. "Will you always be one step ahead of me?"

She blinked up at him and grinned. "Only if you want me to," she said. "If you prefer me beside you, that would be okay as well. I just don't do the *following* thing."

He wrapped his arms around her. "You can lead anytime." He flipped himself down, spread-eagled on the bed, and added, "Especially right now."

She burst out laughing, once again straddling his hips, and noted, "Our laughter is something I really love about us. We share so much joy."

"That's a good thing, and that's something we can build on too."

"Love it," she murmured, as her hands explored the massive chest in front of her and the abs that tightened under her fingers. She giggled as he shifted away from her, her glance lightning quick as she asked, "Are you ticklish?"

"Yeah, I might be a little." He gasped as she slid a hand down the inside of his thigh to his knee, where he twitched again.

She chuckled.

Wallace warned her, "Remember now that two can play that game."

She wrinkled up her nose. "*Ugh.* I am terribly ticklish."

"*Ha,* so you know what that means."

"Yep, I sure do," she declared. "It means, *no tickling.*"

And, with a sigh, she stroked and explored every inch of his big legs, taut muscles, smooth skin covered in dark hair, even his feet. By the time she made her way back up to his hips, he shifted on the bed, easing her toward the place that he most wanted her to explore.

She looked down at the erection standing proud in front

of her and smiled. "And then there's this."

As she wrapped her hand around it and gently stroked it up and down, he sucked in his breath, his hips reaching up, plunging deeper into her grasp. "Yeah, there is that," he noted, moaning and grunting. "It needs a little attention."

"Does it?" she murmured, as she looked at it, now chuckling. "Looks pretty happy to me." She stroked it several more times, letting her fingers slide over the tip, and then she glanced up at him, leaned over, and kissed the top. Almost instantly she was flipped onto her back, and, with a shriek of laughter, she found him suddenly on top of her.

"You know, the teasing is one thing, and maybe tomorrow, maybe next week, maybe a year from now, I'll be totally fine with it," he shared, smiling, as he settled himself between her thighs. "But right now, hell no. I've been wanting to do this for way too long."

"Oh, I doubt it. I think this is just a new thing for you," she teased, shifting beneath him.

"No, not at all," he countered. "Besides, I'm not exactly sure what *new* means in your book," he added, "but I'm sure you noticed our energy right from the moment we met."

She nodded. "I did."

"I'm sure you noticed our energy when I found you."

She smiled, her gaze heating up, and she nodded. "I did."

"And I'm sure you can feel our joint energy right now."

She chuckled, wrapping her arms around his neck, and whispered, "Oh, I definitely do." Because, in truth, there was this twisting, twining energy wrapped around them in a classic lovers' embrace.

She shifted her hands to his buttocks, then rearranged her own hips, wrapping her thighs tightly around him.

Whispering, she added, "I really do think it's time for you to come home."

He groaned at her words and, with one deft plunge, seated himself deep inside her. He raised himself up on his arms, his eyes closed as he shuddered. "Jesus, I don't know whether it's the energy or ..."

"I don't need an explanation either way," she muttered. "For God's sake, just move."

And with a smile that quickly turned to a groan, he started to move, increasing the pace, plunge after plunge, until she cried out, her world coming apart in waves. He followed soon afterward, collapsing beside her and rolling over to hold her close. He kissed her once and, with a big sigh, suggested, "Nap time?"

She chuckled. "Only for a moment. Then after that, I suggest we go for round two."

He pulled her closer and whispered, "I'm game, if you are, but remember that we have all the time we need."

"Yeah, we have time," she agreed, "but I don't want to waste any more of it."

Wrapping her arms around his neck, she pulled him down for another deep kiss, knowing that her future had never looked brighter.

EPILOGUE

TERK PICKED UP his favorite mug and filled it with coffee, then grabbed a second mug and filled it as well. With both cups in hand, he headed over to a couple easy chairs that sat in front of the fireplace. He handed one coffee cup to Jonas.

Jonas accepted it gratefully. "It's a hell of a spot to be in," he muttered, taking a sip, then sinking into the chair, cuddling in against the fireplace. "Life is pretty tough here for you guys, isn't it?"

"Let's just say, we've come through the worst of it, and we're pretty happy where we've landed," Terk clarified in a somewhat neutral tone.

Jonas gave him a sideways look. "I do understand, you know?"

"Good," Terk replied, "because most of us have been to hell and back, so trust doesn't come that easy."

"Right, I understand that too," he murmured, "and, in many cases, with good reason."

"What about you? Did you find more moles?"

"We did," he admitted in an abashed tone. "Unfortunately another guy in MI5 was working with the new hire in MI6," he added, with a wave of his hand. "We figure more snitches are on the payroll at the hotels we are known to use, so we're following up on all that too. Regardless, with both of our inhouse moles tossed out, we're hoping for an easier time going forward."

"Until the next one."

Jonas nodded, as he stared down at his cup. "The sad thing is, there's always a next one, isn't there?"

Terk looked over at him and nodded. "There is. We keep thinking that we're finally at a stage where everything will be fine. Then something happens, and it's not fine anymore."

"And here I was hoping you had good news."

"Oh, I have lots of good news, just not necessarily anything that matters to you," Terk noted. "I get that you're here for healing, and believe me that the gals will do the best they can for you. However, I feel as if something else is behind your visit—something deeper."

Jonas looked around to see if anyone was nearby. "You asked me to look into a certain matter a while back."

Terk shifted and straightened. "I did."

"I've got some interesting information."

"What's that?"

"The private investigator hired to look into the case was murdered not long after starting the investigation."

Terk frowned at him. "That's not in my files."

"No, that's because the family didn't want it made public."

"Yet that's a big point in terms of what happened to Riff's fiancée. That PI was the one actively trying to find out what happened to her. So, if he was murdered and not killed in a car accident, as Riff was told, that's a big deal."

"He was run over in a deliberate act, but there are no answers, no leads. We have nothing to point to who did it."

"That makes me wonder if it was a professional hit."

"Oh, don't worry. It makes me wonder the same thing," Jonas confirmed. "I get that it's very important, and, for some people involved, like Riff, it's beyond important. But that PI case was closed, and nobody's willing to open it because it's already been assessed and declared an accident. However, a new look says it's a deliberate hit-and-run. We also have a family member saying they received a threatening letter that, if they pursued this any further, somebody else in the family would die."

"*Great*," Terk muttered. "So, chances are, the private eye was on to something."

"Exactly. So, what I do have, I admit it's not a whole lot," Jonas conceded, as he reached into his pocket and pulled out a USB key. "This is what we found on the investigator's computer at the time of his death."

Terk reached out a hand, taking the key, and nodded. "Thank you, Jonas."

"I don't know that it will be of any help."

"No, but, if it gives us even one more little bit of information, it's important. No matter how small, it's still a piece of the puzzle, and we need it."

At that moment, Riff walked in, his gaze going to the two of them. He joined them, frowning, looking down at Jonas's leg. "How bad is it?"

"It will be fine, given a little time," Jonas replied, with a formal tone. "Thanks for the assistance in the tunnel."

Riff nodded. "No problem. That's the way the world is supposed to work, right?"

At that, Terk held out his hand with the USB key. "Riff, Jonas came for a little healing assistance, but he also brought this for you."

Riff stared at it, as if it would bite him. He looked from

one man to the other and back again cautiously, as if he knew already. "What is it?"

Jonas replied, "It's the contents of the private eye's personal effects and computer files and diary at the time of his murder."

It took Riff a few minutes to blink his way through that. "*Murder*. It was declared an accident."

"That's how the family wanted it portrayed and reported. I spoke with them recently, and they received a death threat in a letter just prior to a public announcement about the loss of their family member. The letter promised the immediate death of another family member if they didn't go along with the accidental death report on the PI and didn't drop all attempts to prove it was anything other than an unfortunate car accident."

He stared at Jonas in shock. "So, you're saying the investigator was murdered."

"That's our belief, yes," Jonas confirmed. "I figured you would want first crack at it."

He snatched the USB key from Terk's hand and stared down at it, his jaw working. Just then Angela walked into the room. He looked over at her. "You always seem to turn up just at the most inconvenient time."

"Or the right time," she argued, staring at the USB key. "Did I just hear what I thought I heard?"

He nodded. "Apparently. ... I don't know what's on here yet." He looked back at Jonas.

Jonas shrugged. "I don't either," he admitted. "But one good turn deserves another, so thank you for keeping me alive back there in the tunnels. I have a hunch you may have done more than just pack me out." When he saw the quick grin cross Riff's face, Jonas nodded. "Let's hope this helps your hunt."

As Riff headed out of the room, he looked back at Terk and announced, "I'll go check this out."

Terk nodded.

Angela rushed to follow Riff, calling out, "Wait for me."

He looked back at her and frowned. "You know you don't need to be involved in this."

She glared at him. "I lost someone too. She was my sister, after all."

He hesitated, then nodded. "Fine, but it's unlikely you'll be happy with anything we find."

"I haven't been happy about anything over the last five years to date," she added bitterly. "So at least let me find some closure."

He hesitated, then turned to Terk, who nodded. Riff sighed. "Fine, but don't blame me if you don't like where this ends up."

"I won't blame you at all," she declared.

He laughed. "That would be a first. So far, you've done nothing but." And, with that, he turned and walked out.

She now cast a glance back at Terk.

Terk again nodded. "If you don't go, you won't ever get answers. If I *must* weigh in, don't let him push you around."

She snorted. "I haven't ever let him push me around so far," she declared. "Damn, I've all but moved into your place, trying to stay close, and all he does is try to push me away."

"He needs answers first," Terk noted, his tone steady as he studied her. "Give him some room but maybe not too much."

She nodded and flashed him a bright grin. "Thanks."

And, with that, she was gone.

Jonas groaned at his side. "Young love. ... Nothing hurts quite like that."

Terk looked over at him and nodded. "Particularly with star-crossed lovers like these two, but maybe now they can finally find some answers about the past and can head into the future."

"I hope so. ... Now, what about you running a government department for me?"

Terk sighed. Jonas was apparently still serious about this, given everything they had been through. "If I take it up with the team and if they all say yes, I *might* be interested," Terk explained. "But you know for a fact that every fricking one of them will say not only no but *hell no*." Then he gave Jonas a fat smile. "Let's just continue the way we are for now. Maybe before long we'll have Riff's case fully closed, and I can get him to come on board full-time."

"He's good, isn't he?" Jonas asked, as he studied the doorway the two had gone through.

"He's one of the best," Terk replied. "He just doesn't believe it. Something, ... well, finding these answers," he added, "will make all the difference."

"I hope so." Jonas looked far off into the distance. "The world is a mess out there, and, if we don't have people like you and me and them to straighten out all the problems, ... it'll only get worse."

And, with that, the two men raised their coffee mugs, clanked them together, and each had a sip. Terk noted, "You know, if you didn't have a busted-up leg, we could be drinking whiskey."

Jonas stared down at his coffee mug and then frowned at him and declared, "I don't have a busted-up leg."

Terk laughed, then got up and grabbed the whiskey bottle from the nearby shelf, quickly pouring a healthy slug into each cup. "Now, let's have some proper coffee."

And together they sat here and enjoyed the moment.

This concludes Book 14 of Terk's Guardians: Wallace.
Read about Riff: Terk's Guardians, Book 15

Terk's Guardians: Riff (Book #15)

At Terk's request, Jonas had discreetly delved into the mystery surrounding the murder of Riff's fiancée and unearthed a crucial piece of information that could shatter the case wide open. For Riff, the frustration involved in finding the murderer is palpable. He would have taken action much sooner, if only this information had come to light earlier. Yet it had been buried in silence, unnoticed, … until now.

Angela had harbored a complex mix of love and resentment for Riff for years. He had been her sister's fiancé, leaving Angela with no choice but to keep her feelings hidden. After her sister's tragic murder, Riff spiraled into darkness, consumed by his quest for answers. Angela sought the truth as well, but she knew that her presence was a painful reminder of his loss—a tension neither of them could ignore.

As the long-buried answers begin to surface, the new information is nothing like what either of them expected, propelling them into a perilous journey toward the truth.

Amid the danger, an unexpected bond forms between them, adding a layer of complexity to their shared mission. Together they must navigate a treacherous path, where every revelation brings them closer to both the truth and each other.

Find Book 15 here!
To find out more visit Dale Mayer's website.
https://geni.us/DMSRiff

Author's Note

Thank you for reading Wallace: Terk's Guardians, Book 14!
If you enjoyed the book, please take a moment and leave a
short review.

Dear reader,

I love to hear from readers, and you can contact me at my
website: www.dalemayer.com or at my Facebook author
page. To be informed of new releases and special offers, sign
up for my newsletter or follow me on BookBub. And if you
are interested in joining Dale Mayer's Reader Group, here is
the Facebook sign up page.
http://geni.us/DaleMayerFBGroup

Cheers,
Dale Mayer

About the Author

Dale Mayer is a *USA Today* best-selling author, best known for her SEALs military romances, her Psychic Visions series, and her Lovely Lethal Garden cozy series. Her contemporary romances are raw and full of passion and emotion (Broken But … Mending, Hathaway House series). Her thrillers will keep you guessing (Kate Morgan, By Death series), and her romantic comedies will keep you giggling (*It's a Dog's Life*, a stand-alone novella; and the Broken Protocols series, starring Charming Marvin, the cat).

Dale honors the stories that come to her—and some of them are crazy, break all the rules and cross multiple genres!

To go with her fiction, she also writes nonfiction in many different fields, with books available on résumé writing, companion gardening, and the US mortgage system. All her books are available in print and ebook format.

Connect with Dale Mayer Online

Dale's Website – www.dalemayer.com
Twitter – @DaleMayer
Facebook Page – geni.us/DaleMayerFBFanPage
Facebook Group – geni.us/DaleMayerFBGroup
BookBub – geni.us/DaleMayerBookbub
Instagram – geni.us/DaleMayerInstagram
Goodreads – geni.us/DaleMayerGoodreads
Newsletter – geni.us/DaleNews